SECRETS ARE NO FUN

D1522257

REBECCA ZEIDMAN

authorHOUSE·

AuthorHouse™
1663 Liberty Drive
Bloomington, IN 47403
www.authorhouse.com
Phone: 833-262-8899

This is a work of fiction. All of the characters, names, incidents, organizations, and dialogue in this novel are either the products of the author's imagination or are used fictitiously.

Published by AuthorHouse 03/09/2023

ISBN: 978-1-6655-7984-1 (sc)
ISBN: 978-1-6655-7982-7 (hc)
ISBN: 978-1-6655-7983-4 (e)

Library of Congress Control Number: 2023900317

Print information available on the last page.

Any people depicted in stock imagery provided by Getty Images are models, and such images are being used for illustrative purposes only. Certain stock imagery © Getty Images.

Author photo by: Rachel Renov Photography
Front cover design by: Rachel Litton

This book is printed on acid-free paper.

For my parents,
Who continue to love and support me every second of every day

DIAGNOSIS

CHAPTER 1

I had a strange feeling on Tuesday when I got home from school. Everything was the same way I had left it before leaving for school that morning. There was just one important thing missing: Mom.

For as long as I could remember Mom was *always* there when I got home from school. And if she wasn't, she at least warned me. I mean, Marta, our Hungarian babysitter, was there for us. But she wasn't as good as Mom because she didn't speak English and she just wasn't Mom.

You see, Mom loved me so much that she even quit her job for me. (Okay, and maybe for my other siblings, too, but I prefer to think she did it just for me). When I was in first grade Mom decided she wouldn't be able to work as a lawyer in the City and be home in time for my brother and me when we got home from school. It was a good thing she realized her *real* job was being my mom because no one else was as good at it.

Anyways, there was no fresh food, which was also strange. Mom was a cooking fanatic. She told me she didn't know how to cook until she married Dad and that he was skinny when she first married him. But he's gained thirty pounds in the past fifteen years, thanks to Mom's cooking.

Mom's able to cook anything you ask her to. Just give her time and she finds at least five perfect recipes. And normally when I get home from school the entire counter is filled with vegetables, fruit, and chicken or meat. It was like having a home-cooked Thanksgiving dinner *every* night, except without the turkey. So I pretty much freaked out once I realized we'd be eating leftovers. And my twin Sam and younger sister Mollie thought it was weird, too.

"Where's dinner?" Sam whined as he walked into the kitchen, letting the swinging door swing right into Mollie.

"You don't need dinner." My sister rubbed her forehead where the door had smacked her. She sat at the dinner table next to Sam. "You could hold the door open for me, you know?"

Sam rolled his eyes and rubbed his belly. My brother was a bit heavy. But he was only eleven, and he didn't have to worry about girls until he was at least twelve. "I'm starving . . . Wait, where's Mom?"

My sister and I looked around the empty kitchen and then at each other. Clearly, she wasn't home, and clearly, there wasn't going to be any dinner. We understood that. Sam didn't. Why did people always say he was the smarter twin? Maybe it was because he was mature for his age or because he wore round glasses that made him look like a chubby version of Harry Potter, but Sam was definitely not smarter than me. Yes, he was better in math. But I was better in English. And to defend my case, Mom told me we even had the same IQ. To me, that sort of made us equal.

"So . . ." I stared at the empty table in front of me before clasping my hands together and resting my head on them. Mollie did the same while Sam got up to look for Marta.

Eventually, Marta came in wearing her usual white sweatshirt and blue jeans. Sighing in relief, my whole body perked up at the thought of dinner. And then she started speaking Hungarian, which I understood as well as a crying baby. "*Vacsora a hűtőben*," Marta said as she opened the fridge.

Lucky for us, this time I did understand what Marta was telling us as she frantically pointed at the stacks of leftovers wrapped neatly in tinfoil: There are leftovers in the fridge . . . Enjoy! She smiled as she took the plates out of the pantry.

Mollie, Sam, and I helped ourselves. We sat and ate chicken and rice in silence before going upstairs and doing homework. Mom hadn't called, and I was becoming worried.

I was concentrating on a math problem when the phone rang. I jumped up from my desk, happy I had an excuse to take a break. I ran for the phone, hoping it was Mom, but my sister grabbed it before me.

I ran across the hall to her room. "Can I please have the phone?" I begged as I pulled the telephone away from her, but she motioned me away and turned her back to me. I kept whining though. "I need to speak to Mom!"

I could tell she wasn't going to give it up. I ran downstairs just as I heard my brother's voice over the intercom. "It's for you, Ari," he said and then hung up.

"Hello?" I picked up the phone in the kitchen. "Mommy? I miss you. How are you?" I asked in the sweetest voice possible. Maybe she would hurry up if she remembered she was coming home to the most perfect daughter on the entire planet.

I heard Dad mumble something in the background. Why was he with her? He should be coming home from work by now not driving somewhere mysterious with Mom.

"Sweetie, I have news," she started.

"OK. What is it?" I asked after Mom paused for what seemed like an eternity.

"I went to the doctor today, and she told me that . . . that I have a boo-boo. Everything is going to be fine . . . but I need surgery. I will be home very soon and explain everything."

"A boo-boo? What kind of surgery? Mom, what's going on?" I demanded. I sat down on the kitchen chair and put my knees to my chest. "Hello?" Why wasn't she answering my questions? I needed to know what she was talking about. My frustration brewing, I tried to breathe and calm down.

But then I heard a beep through the phone, which meant one of my annoying siblings had just come on the line to interrupt my conversation with Mom. So I put my head down on the kitchen table. My head was swimming, and I couldn't deal with my eight-year-old sister's voice whining to Mom about why she wasn't home yet. I slammed the phone down and let out a deep breath.

I did have a valid reason for needing silence and for needing Mom, who had just told me she was at a doctor and needed surgery, by the way. Well, to be specific, she said she had a "boo-boo." What in the world was a "boo-boo" if not a scrape? I got scrapes on my knees all the time, and I didn't need surgery to help me feel better. I needed a Band-Aid!

"Ugh," I said to no one in particular. I stomped my foot and ran through the swinging door letting it swing behind me. I ran up the steps to my room and tripped on my way. I stayed on the itchy carpet, and then I cried, putting my face in my hands, trying to hold myself together.

I picked up my head for a second and looked in the mirror hanging across from the staircase. I had big messy curls that framed my small, pale face and a freckled, crooked nose. My face was red, splotchy, and tear-stained, and I hated that I was crying.

Three years ago I had sat crying with my face in my hands just like this, except it was when Mom told me Zeide passed away. I hadn't even realized he was Dad's stepfather until after he was gone. I always thought I was lucky to have three amazing grandfathers. He'd always let me braid his beard, wash his bald head, and paint his nails pink.

That day Mom came in with my aunt, Mimi, and sat Sam, Mollie, and me on the couch. She told us what had happened—that Zeide died in his sleep, and it didn't hurt. It was very early in the morning, way before school started, and I remember thinking how scary it would be to die in your sleep. Right away, Mollie cried and freaked out, running away from all of us. Mom ran after her, leaving Sam and me with Mimi. Sam sat and stared sadly. He looked like a statue. And I cried in my hands and didn't move.

Sitting in the same position as I had then, I wondered why Mom told us about Zeide while we were sitting all together and not on the phone. Zeide dying and Mom's boo-boo—whatever it was—were both bad news. This time, though, it felt different.

I was crying about something that was *going* to happen in the future. It was a pending doom, like a ticking time bomb. It was bound to explode, leaving my family and me in the wake of destruction. How could anyone clean up such a mess? How could life go back to normal after something called a boo-boo?

I mean, the doctors would have to cut Mom open. She would be sleeping, of course, so it wouldn't hurt. But how could *my* mom have something wrong with her?

I looked in the mirror again and willed myself to breathe. *In and out.* I felt better after I wiped my tears and pulled my hair into a ponytail. I needed to calm down.

Between breaths, it dawned on me that I didn't even know what Mom was talking about. She never answered my questions, and I could have been overreacting about her boo-boo after all. Maybe the doctor made a mistake and told Mom the wrong diagnosis. Maybe there was no boo-boo or surgery at all.

I felt better as I walked upstairs to my room, all the while convincing myself that this boo-boo had been a misunderstanding that would be worked out in the morning. I pretended not to hear my sister's whimpering and shoved down any guilt I had about not comforting her. Most of all I held back any temptation to see how Sam was doing. Since he was the type of kid who thought nothing bad ever happened in the world, he'd be crushed if something were actually wrong with Mom. I didn't have the strength to face my thoughts—let alone watch my siblings break down. I convinced myself that this was the only way I would get through the night. Well, at least until Mom got home.

CHAPTER 2

For a split second as I got ready for bed, I blamed everything on myself. It was my fault Mom had a boo-boo.

Two years ago, I was in Chicago for my cousin's Bat Mitzvah. My entire family was sitting in my cousin's apartment eating dinner. It was nice when we all got together. Since I had a really small family everyone was super close. Things usually became hectic, though, mostly because all the children were little, my cousins had a crazy dog, and everyone was excited to see each other. Still, no matter how chaotic things got, we always made the best out of our get-togethers. After all, it was these occasions that we'd remember for the rest of our lives.

Well, I remembered that one.

I was playing with my cousin when their babysitter walked by. She didn't speak English, only Hungarian, so for some odd reason, I thought it would be funny to say, "You are so ugly. How can you look at yourself in the mirror every single day?"

The truth was, Merieca (the babysitter) wasn't even ugly. Yes, she wore enormous plastic glasses that magnified her eyes to the size of Earth, but everyone knew a key ingredient to an extreme makeover is contact lenses, so why couldn't Merieca just get with the program? And it wasn't any of my business if she wanted to brush her hair or not.

I was never one of those kids who teased people for fun, so some other force of nature *must* have made me say what I'd said. It was probably that same force of nature that made the babysitter miraculously understand English. After that, everything became frenzied. Mom yelled at me until her face turned completely purple, and I cried so loud the neighbors probably heard me. This was how it went:

Mom: "How could you ever say those words to a person?"

Me: "How could I *ever* have known that she would understand English? I never heard her say an English word in my life."

Mom: "It doesn't matter. That is not how I want you to talk to people. Don't you agree, David?"

Dad: "Come on, Ari, you know you should never speak like that to anyone."

Me: "Honestly, I didn't know that she would tell on me."

Mom: "But how could you even say that to someone?"

Me: "You told me never to lie. Could I really get punished for being honest?"

Well, it went on for hours. We yelled in the house. We yelled in the streets back to the hotel. We yelled until Mom burst: "You can't use your computer for two weeks or your phone. And I swear on *my* life that you will never forget the way you embarrassed me tonight and the horrible way you behaved in front of our entire family."

I was quiet after that.

Mom had sworn on her life. To me, it meant if I didn't remember what I did that night in Chicago, she would die. It was a little crazy to think Mom's life was in my hands, but I was a little girl then. I needed to give myself a break.

But I didn't forget what had happened in Chicago, which meant I didn't break Mom's swear. Though I knew her having a boo-boo wasn't my fault, I still cried.

It was the first time in my life I cried. Sure, I *had* cried because of a low test grade or because a friend was mean. But this time was different. I cried because I had a real reason to cry. I felt something deep within. Maybe it was a ball of water, but it was something I needed to get out. I had a gut feeling this wasn't just a boo-boo. This was serious. This scared me.

I got into bed and wrapped myself in my cozy pink blanket pretending it was Mom hugging me. Still, it wasn't the same as having her there.

Nothing was.

CHAPTER 3

I threw my blanket on the floor and flopped up and down in bed. Sitting up, I leaned against my hard headboard and crossed my arms over my chest. It was ten o'clock at night, and Mom *just* called to tell me she was almost home but stuck in traffic. I guess that explained where she had been the past few hours, but what about the entire afternoon?

I just had to breathe and let it go. If Mom had a boo-boo then she had every right to miss one dinner. It shouldn't be the end of the world. Though to me, it was. I tried to think about something else that would help calm me down. The first thing that popped into my head was the first day of fifth grade.

I was nervous. Everyone knows fifth grade is a hard year. That's why before I stepped onto the school bus on my very first day, Mom gave me an extra big hug. I definitely could handle the homework. Spelling tests were easy and math problems can be solved—especially after asking my genius brother for help. But there were a couple of things I just couldn't handle, and that's what made me so nervous.

Boys. It wasn't usually a problem. I attended The Jewish Academy of Atlantic Beach, a Jewish day school in New York, so naturally, the boys and girls were kept separate. Boys were on one side and girls were on the other. Things were good that way. Everyone knew where to go and who to be friends with, and it was never a problem. But last summer Eva became boy-crazy, and little by little everyone in my class seemed to have caught the bug. That's what Eva always did. She made a big deal about something and then got everyone in on it.

Let's take her hairstyle, for example. Eva takes the front of her hair, poofs it up to the sky, and then clips it to hold her hair in place. This hairstyle made her look *at least* three inches taller, and she got everyone to wear their hair that way. I didn't know why things happened like that, but that's how things worked in elementary school. I was thankful to have Hailey as my best friend because together we could make everyone realize Eva wasn't so special and boys came from Jupiter.

Honestly, I shouldn't be afraid of talking to boys because they are *very* similar to girls, but I was completely and totally scared. The weirdest part was I often had boys at my house because Sam always had his friends over. And most of the time they even slept over, so I had the perfect opportunity to socialize. But I just couldn't seem to get the hang of talking to them. And it was even worse that the boys he brought over saw me in the morning right after I woke up when I had bad breath and messy hair. And sometimes they *even* got front-row seats to a fight between Mom and me. I should have felt comfortable in front of them. But I didn't.

I sat back down on my bed and threw my body backward, letting out a deep sigh. "I can't believe I did that," I squealed. Embarrassing encounters between me and Sam's friends flashed through my mind, like the time Mollie and I put a show on in our basement without realizing all of Sam's friends were secretly watching.

As all my problems swarmed in my head, I groaned and put my head face down on my pillow, breathing heavily and letting all my frustration seep out. I opened my eyes at the pink fabric and stared. Pink, yellow, and green shapes—squares, triangles, and stars—appeared and danced around my vision. The thought of my eyes playing tricks on me always made me laugh.

Turning on my side, I remembered the worst part of the year was that we'd be watching the most horrifying movie in the entire universe: the *Period Movie*. It's a movie about how your body changes and how to stay healthy and, most importantly, to maintain good hygiene. I mean, how many ways can you say you're going to grow breasts and hair in different places without making kids laugh uncomfortably? Add in the fact my teacher was going to watch it with us and I think I could safely say the hour-long movie would officially become the worst hour of my life.

I threw my hands to my head, officially frustrated. Thinking about the movie made me hot, so I got up and opened the window. That's when I heard a car door close and the beep of a car locking. My entire body perked up.

Mom was home.

"MOM!" I ran to the top of the staircase and looked down.

She was standing in the doorway taking off her shoes. Dad came in behind her looking more tired than he did after a long day of work. He loosened his tie and walked to the dining room where I assumed he would sort through the day's mail.

"Hi, sweetie." Mom looked up the stairs at me. She looked like she'd been crying, too. "I'm sorry I'm so late. Go to sleep, please. We'll talk in the morning. I love you."

And for some reason, I didn't fight her. Maybe I was happy she was home or maybe I was just tired of crying or maybe I felt bad for her that she had been crying. Either way, I went back to bed and stared at the ceiling for another hour. I tried not to think about boo-boos or fifth grade or boys or periods or anything that would make me nervous. Instead, I came up with a plan: find out about Mom's boo-boo.

CHAPTER 4

"What's your boo-boo?" I asked Mom the next morning.

I didn't want to waste any time with Mission Find Out About Mom's Boo-Boo. So I woke up anticipating some answers. I had gotten dressed extra quickly to save time to talk to Mom, and I didn't have time to work on taming my hair. Now it looked like a bird had made a nest on top of my head.

"Good morning, Ari." Mom looked at me from under the covers.

"Hi, kiddo," Dad said as he tucked his shirt into his pants. When he looked up at me, he raised his eyebrows. "You look different today. Did you sleep last night?"

It was true. Besides the obvious hair problem, my eyes were so puffy it looked like I had been crying for a week, and my face was a red pudgy ball.

"Well, I was crying last night. You would know too if you had been home." I made a face at Dad. Then I turned to Mom. "Can you tell me what a boo-boo means, please?" I stomped my feet and sat down on the spinning chair.

"I already told you, nothing that you should worry about," Mom said as she picked up the remote control and turned the TV on. The sound of the news reporters' voices filled the room.

"Are you serious?" I put my hand on my hip. It was a little too early to give Mom an attitude. But she should be thankful that she'd skipped out on it last night.

"Arianna, give Mom a break for now. We love you," Dad piped in.

"Whatever." I rolled my eyes. I got up to kiss Mom on the forehead. "Bye."

"Have a great day at school, Ari," they called after me.

I walked across the street to the bus stop in the most annoyed mood in the world. Sam asked what was wrong, but I ignored him. It was mostly weird because I was usually the happiest person in the morning. I was a ray of sunshine.

Not this morning.

I got on the bus extra irritated. It had come five minutes late. That's five minutes extra standing in the cold December air with the seemingly harmless first graders who lived on my block.

"Why does your face look like that, Arianna?" Isabella asked. She was a foot shorter than me, her backpack had a huge Hello Kitty on it, and the pallet expander in her mouth made her smile seem extra wide. Normally, I thought she was a cute first-grader who thought I was really cool and complimented my shoes. But today she had nothing nice to say, so she was just the annoying little kid who woke up this morning with the sole purpose of making my life miserable.

Once I was on the bus I took my usual seat next to Hannah, my Bus Buddy. Normally, we talked the entire way to school, but this morning I wasn't in the mood. I stared at the disgusting piece of tape on the seat in front of me. And even if Hannah could tell something was wrong, she never asked. I was not about to vent to my Bus Buddy.

Hannah and I had been sitting together on the bus since first grade. That very first day of first grade I was just as cute and harmless as Isabella seemed to be, and I was really scared to go to elementary school. When I got on the bus and saw that another first-grade girl was there too, I felt safe. Hannah and I promised we'd sit next to each other every single day for the rest of our lives. That meant when we were old and wrinkled and took the city bus to the market, we would sit next to each other. So we spent a lot of time together—a whole fifteen minutes every morning and afternoon.

But I wasn't telling Hannah about Mom. I wasn't telling anybody. My friends would think I was the girl with the sick mom and treat me differently. They would probably give me extra snacks at lunch or let me win our class card game tournaments. I didn't want any of that. I didn't want extra attention because Mom was sick. So I wasn't telling any of my friends. Not Hannah. Not even Hailey.

By the time I got to school, I felt a little better, and I was ready to look normal again, too. The first step: fix my hair. I ran straight to the bathroom the minute I got to school and checked the mirror.

"Oh. My. God." I jumped back from the mirror. My hair was not only frizzy, but it was flat at the top, where I had tried to pat it down that morning, and extended outward at the bottom. Honestly, I could've been mistaken for an extra in an 80's movie.

I ran to class, ducking my head the entire way and hoping no one would see me in the hallway. Thankfully, when I get there Hailey was already sitting at her desk, which was next to mine.

"Hey," I said propping myself on the edge of her desk. "Can you braid my hair, please?"

"Duh. Side or straight?" Hailey sat up, walked behind me, and separated different strands of my thick, frizzy hair. "Why does it look different today, Ari? Did you try a new gel again?"

I was always trying out new products to make my hair less frizzy, and most of the time the gel ended up making my hair look worse. "Not this time, Hailey. I didn't have time to do my hair this morning. Just try to make it look normal, please."

"I don't have to do much to make it look better." She divided my hair into three parts and got to work.

"Thanks." I giggled. I tried not to yelp while she pulled my hair in all different directions, but I couldn't prevent myself from getting teary-eyed.

"This is going to look much better," Hailey said as she added the finishing touches.

"It better," I mumbled as she pulled my hair a little too hard.

"Done." She tied the remaining strands with a hair-tie and exclaimed, "*Voila!*" Facing me now, Hailey said, "You, Ari, just got Hailo'd."

I laughed. Since Hailey's hair expertise was as good as the braiders from @pleasemakemeabraid on Instagram and she knew it, Hailey referred to her clients as being Hailo'd. After Hailey was finished with you, it was as if you had a halo on your head.

"Hailey, that term will *never* catch on."

"It's not my fault that you look like an angel, Ari." Then she made a circle with her fingers and placed it above my head, pretending I was actually an angel. After about a minute of singing, "Ahhhh," Hailey finally pointed to herself and laughed, "Actually, it is!"

Rolling my eyes, I touched the top of my head and felt that it was flat. I ran my hand down my braid and could already feel that it looked *so* much better. I let out a sigh and said, "Thank god."

"I told you," she said as she fanned herself with her hands. "I am the hair goddess."

"You are so dramatic," I rolled my eyes again.

"Don't you know, Ari, that's why you love me," Hailey joked as she organized her desk for first period. "But are you sure you don't want me to make you an Eva poof?" Hailey asked while pointing to a group of girls in the corner who were all sporting the infamous hairdo.

I quickly pushed her hand down. "Stop pointing!" I whispered, "Eva can see everything."

"There's no way you can *see* the board sitting behind someone with that poof." She opened her eyes wide at Eva and the girls in the corner. She looked at me with even wider eyes, "I'm pointing with my eyes."

We laughed until our bellies hurt and until the poof-girls looked back at us. I bet they thought we were talking about how good they looked. We quickly turned away from them and continued laughing.

At my school, we were taught Judaic subjects in the morning by Mrs. Harbor. This included the Hebrew language and Tanakh, our Hebrew bible, which includes all of the famous stories like the splitting of the Red Sea, Yonah and the whale, and love poems between God and His people.

Mrs. Harbor came into the classroom and told us to sit down. We had been learning all about the miracles that happened to the Jews in Egypt. I didn't pay attention to anything that was going on during her lesson. I spent the entire class laughing silently and sitting on my knees. I couldn't see the board because a poof-girl was sitting right in front of me.

After recess, we switched teachers, and Mr. Dawn came into the class. He taught us our English subjects, including English language, social studies, and basic sciences. Normally, he looked like Goofy—with big ears, big eyes, and a big nose. His two front teeth were smaller than the rest of his teeth, so when he smiled I always looked away because it was just too funny.

Today, his mouth was in a straight line, so I had no problem looking at him. "Has anyone heard the phrase, 'A picture is worth a thousand words?'" He slammed his books down on his desk. The noise made my stomach flip. He quickly scribbled the quote on the SMART Board.

I looked at Hailey and whispered, "What's going on?" She shrugged.

Mr. Dawn walked through the rows of desks. He waved his hands in the air as he spoke and opened his eyes wide. If I didn't know Mr. Dawn, I would've thought he had come straight from the nuthouse. He continued, "Girls, you can learn so much about yourselves if you just draw it on a piece of paper!" He said it as if it was the most obvious thing in the world. He clapped his hands and my stomach flipped again. "From now on, we're going to spend a couple of minutes every day drawing a picture." He looked around at our faces to see if any of us understood. I didn't, but I guess he didn't get *that* picture. And with a final clap of his hands, he exclaimed, "Let's get started!"

He pointed to all our notebooks. "Take out a piece of paper and draw a picture of your favorite place to hang out. It could be the ice cream shop, your room, or even school. I have crayons on my desk so take what you want. You should feel like you are being transported to this place as you draw it. *Be* in the picture." He jumped up and down as if he was hopping into Mary Poppin's magical, chalk-drawn sidewalk. "Afterwards, I want you to write one paragraph about what this place means to you and how it reflects the original quote." He tapped his knuckles on the board, finally getting to the point. "Girls, you have an hour."

I ripped out a piece of paper from my pink notebook and started to think. I looked at everyone around me and wondered what each girl would come up with. Hailey was going to draw a picture of her bubby's house. She loved going there because her bubby always made cookies, and she lived by a pretty lake.

I tapped my pencil against my mouth and chewed on the pink eraser. I stopped once I realized I was going to need that eraser.

I couldn't think of one place I liked being. I loved to dance, but I also loved to eat. I loved to read by the beach, but I also loved swimming in the pool. There just wasn't one thing. How could Mr. Dawn tell me to choose one place?

And then it hit me. I felt it as hard as a soccer ball flying at my stomach. It was painful and the feeling stayed there for a while. The place I always loved, whether it was morning or night, was with Mom. I dropped my pencil on my desk and walked out of class.

CHAPTER 5

"Hi, Mom. I'm home!" I yelled throughout the house while slamming the door closed. My teacher told me it was a *mitzvah*, the Hebrew phrase for a good deed, to let your parents know when you arrived home from school. They didn't tell me how it should be done, so I yelled at the top of my lungs. If it bothered Mom she never showed it, so I took it as a good sign.

"Hi, Ari, how was your day?" She came out of the kitchen holding a spoon in her hand. "Actually, can you do me a favor?"

I slumped my backpack on the floor with a thud as a nice way to tell her that all I wanted was to sit down. She didn't get the hint.

"Can you run to my car and get my green, marble notebook? I brought it to the doctor yesterday, and I forgot to bring it inside with me."

Since Mom said, "doctor," I perked up and ran straight back out into the cold. But then I remembered I needed to grab Mom's car keys and a jacket, so I quickly ran back inside. The universe was always slowing me down!

This was my chance to find out what was wrong with Mom once and for all. She knew she couldn't keep anything from me. She was dealing with *her* genes. She was smart, and Dad was smart, and since I was a combination of the two, then I was just short of being a genius.

I ran down my front lawn, unlocked the car, and opened the door. There it was. The minute I saw it I could have sworn hallelujah bells were playing in the background as if I had hit the jackpot. I picked up The Green Notebook and looked at it for a few extra seconds, partly for dramatic effect and partly because I was terrified of what I would see inside.

But I wasn't a procrastinator. I was one of those kids who "ripped everything off like a Band-Aid." I didn't like to prolong the inevitable, and if The Green Notebook was going to give me bad news, well then bring it on.

I turned the first page. I shut my eyes. I opened them. It read:

THE GUIDE TO BREAST CANCER: HOW TO TREAT YOUR DISEASE

OH. MY. GOD. Mom had breast cancer.

How was that possible? How could she call that a boo-boo? People died from that disease every day. I knew that because I watched the news all the time with Mom, and they always showed the families of cancer victims. And the fact they used the term "survivor" for those who had cancer meant it was a big deal if you were still alive after beating cancer.

I was steaming mad. If I were a cartoon, steam would be blowing from my nose and ears, and fire would be escaping from my skull. But this was real life, and now I had to deal with breast cancer.

I felt like screaming. Mom lied to me and told me she had a boo-boo. Cancer was no boo-boo. It was a disease. A real life-threatening, life-sucking, life-killing disease!

I ran inside. I slammed the door. I heard a cracking sound that told me I had broken the door. I ignored it and yelled, "I'm back!"

"Did you get the book?" Mom came out of the kitchen acting like nothing was wrong.

"Why didn't you tell me?" I cried.

My mom looked at my face and the notebook in my hand. She didn't say a word.

"You lied to me, Mom." She rushed to me and put her hands on my shoulders as I continued to cry. "You are sick. Very sick! You are going to be like all the other people who have cancer. You are going to *die*, Mom!" I slumped down onto the black and white marbled floor and put my face into my hands. They were still cold from being outside.

"Sweetie," I felt Mom's arms around me. She smelled like food. She always did when she was cooking. "I'm not dying. Having cancer doesn't mean that there is no hope. Sometimes the doctors find it so late that there is nothing left to do but help make the person, um… feel more comfortable. But the doctors found my cancer early. Do you know what that means, Ari?"

I shook my head. My mom continued as she wiped my tears, "It means, that I'm going to have surgery, and we're hoping they can take it out of me."

I looked up at her and saw that her eyes were watery, but tears weren't rolling down her cheeks. "But I saw it on TV. Katie Couric's husband died of cancer. We watched it on the news together. Don't you remember?" I sniffled, and my eyes burned. Katie Couric's husband was the only person I could name that had cancer.

"Arianna, I believe that I can beat this, and so does your father. Now, I need you to believe in me too. Can you do that for me?" Mom shook my shoulders to help rile me up.

"I can do that." This was starting to seem like a cheerleading squad, and if this was our first pep rally, I wasn't going to disappoint. "You can do it, Mom."

Her entire face lifted into a smile. She tucked my hair behind my ears and said softly, "I just need you to keep this a secret from Sam and Mollie. I don't want them to worry." She wiped my tears with her hands and pulled me up from the floor.

I looked at my beautiful mom. She had lush, dark hair and huge, brown eyes. How could someone so beautiful be sick? I loved her, and because I loved her so much, I told her I would keep it a secret.

"Come, Ari." She took my hand and led me to the kitchen. "I tried a new chicken recipe for dinner, and I also made broccoli."

"You know I hate chicken," I stopped in my tracks. After finding out such bad news, I at least expected my favorite dish for dinner.

"Tomorrow night. I promise. Come." She motioned me to follow her into the kitchen, but I hesitated. "Sam's not going to be home for a while, he's at hockey practice. Mollie's at a friend doing a project." Mom looked at the clock to make sure it wasn't time to pick her up yet. "I have over an hour. I can sit with you while you eat. It'll be me and you."

That, I couldn't resist.

Once I was comfortably sitting at the table picking at the ugly placemats we'd been using since I was six years old, Mom asked, "So when's your next spelling test, Ari?"

Mom always helped my brother and me with our homework. She sometimes typed notes for Sam, and she gave me practice spelling tests so when I took the real ones I always did very well.

"You're worrying about that now?" I was confused.

"Yes. My boo-boo will not affect how well you do in school. This is not a get-out-of-school-free card." She always knew exactly what I was thinking.

Mom put a plate of chicken and broccoli in front of me and sat down. I took my first bite of chicken, and it was yummy. I tried to hide the fact I liked it, though. I didn't want her to start making chicken all the time.

"It's next Thursday. And I don't need your help this time," I answered while chewing a big piece of broccoli.

"So then do you want to snuggle and watch TV until I have to get Mollie?" Mom put on the cutest face she was capable of making. I laughed because I was the one who taught her how to make such a cute face.

"Let me finish this, and I'll race you upstairs." I swallowed the last piece of chicken so fast I almost choked. "But only if we don't have to watch one of those lawyer shows."

When I was little, I was afraid of the dark, and for some reason, I thought monsters lived under my bed, so I insisted on sleeping with my parents. They always thought I was sleeping, but there was no way I was able to fall asleep that quickly, especially when the TV was blasting and I was squished in between them.

The entire time they thought I was sleeping I was watching TV with them. And what I realized was that grown-up TV shows were boring. They were either about lawyers or people looking for serial killers. And I was not interested in either of those.

"You got it." Mom smiled and squeezed my hand.

CHAPTER 6

After I found out Mom had cancer I felt better because I was in on the big secret, but I couldn't help feeling guilty for keeping it from Mollie and Sam.

When Sam got back from hockey practice that night he came into my room and sat on my purple couch. I knew he wanted to talk about something, but for some reason his vocal cords stopped working—words were not coming out of his mouth. He just sat there and stared.

"Are you okay?" I broke the silence, even though he was the one who came into my room and interrupted my concentration on a very difficult math problem.

Sam squirmed. "Why wouldn't I be okay?"

I yawned and leaned back in my chair to stretch my arms. "I don't think that's such a crazy question, Sam. You just came in here and started staring at my wall." I pointed at the blank white wall in front of him.

"I didn't know that walls got offended when you stared at them."

"What are you talking about?" I was not in the right state of mind to start playing mind games with Sam. I needed to get to the point. "So, are you going to tell me what's wrong or am I going to have to wrestle it out of you?" I leaned over and gave him a playful punch on the shoulder.

But Sam didn't think it was so playful. "Why are you hitting me?" He leaned away from me and held onto his shoulder as if he was in pain.

"I barely touched you!" I said loudly. "It was playful. I swear!"

"Stop yelling at me."

"I am not yelling, Sam. Please calm down." I stood up from my chair and slowly walked closer to him.

"Yes, you are. You *are* screaming." Sam's face turned a dark shade of red, and I saw green veins popping out from his neck. I took a step back.

"I am just trying to help, Sam. I want to know what's wrong."

Sam looked down at his hands and then up at me. I didn't think he was here to fight, but it was ingrained in our DNA to bicker whenever there was a chance. That's what siblings did.

"Sam," I spoke extra calmly, deciding to be the more mature one and take it down a notch. "Are you going to tell me what's wrong?"

"Nothing's wrong, Ari." Then he got up and stomped to my door. "Why does everyone keep asking me that?"

"I'm just asking you a question," I said to him, my hands in front of my chest as a defense.

"I am most definitely calm," he said and then slammed my door behind him as he left the room, proving the exact opposite of what he was saying. He was most definitely *not* calm.

"You've got to be kidding me," I said to myself, sitting back in my chair and swiveling forward to face my unfinished math homework. I needed to get it done correctly especially since I didn't have my genius brother at my side to help me anymore.

"What happened?" Dad was poking his head through a crack in the door. "What did you do to Sam?"

Swiveling my chair back around, I defended myself. "I didn't do anything. He just came in and started yelling."

"Are you sure?" Dad's eyes bulged. "He said you punched him."

"It was a friendly punch!" I threw my hands in the air. "Come on, would I lie?"

"All right. I'll go talk to him." Dad smiled at me. "Good night, kiddo."

"Night," I said trying to return my focus to math, but I couldn't. I hated fractions. I hated math. And I hated this secret. Why couldn't Dad or Mom tell Sam what was going on?

Poor Sam was coming to *me* to give him some advice. I bet he couldn't even see through his glasses because they were all foggy from crying. And the worst part was that Sam didn't even know what he was crying about.

I couldn't believe I was ever happy to be in the Loop of Trust between Mom and me. Secrets were *not* fun. Not one bit.

I looked at the digital clock on my shelf. It was 9:32 pm. It was definitely too late to start failing at the next set of math problems. As I closed my textbook, I convinced myself I was done studying for the night.

Deciding Sam was Dad's problem, I walked across the hall to Mollie's room. I could at least try to be there for her even if I couldn't tell her the truth.

"Hey," I said as I opened her door a bit.

"Hey, Ari." Mollie was already in bed reading a book, tucked under the fluffiest blanket on earth.

"Hi, Ari," I heard Mom's voice and opened the door fully. Mom was sitting on the couch across from Mollie reading a magazine. She was wearing an old Columbia Law t-shirt and sweatpants and her curly hair was in a bun. I was happy she looked relaxed.

"I didn't know everyone was in here," I said excitedly as I hopped in bed with Mollie. I threw her book on the ground, ignoring Mollie's irritated glance.

Mom frowned. "You better pick that up before you leave."

"Obviously. What's everyone doing?" I looked from Mom to Mollie. I curled up next to Mollie and wrapped my arm around her, making myself as comfortable as possible. Mollie suffered from a severe case of Invasion of Personal Space Syndrome and was not smiling. But I didn't care. She was adorable.

"Do you have to be on top of me?" She tried to push me away, but it only made me hold on tighter.

"We're just reading. It's time for Mollie to go to sleep," Mom said looking at her watch. She got up and walked to Mollie's side of the bed.

"Give us five minutes," I begged Mom and put on my cute face.

Mom looked at Mollie, who smiled. I knew she wanted to spend time with me. "Just five minutes, please." Mollies big brown eyes widened, and she pushed out her lower lip.

Mom couldn't resist. "Five minutes and then lights out girls. I'll be back to check on you two soon."

"Love you," we called as she left the room.

"So," I said propping myself up with my elbow, "what's up?"

"I made a diorama for school today," Mollie told me.

"You made diarrhea for school? How is your teacher going to grade that?" I asked putting my fingers up to my nose and waving my hands in the air as if to push away the smell.

Mollie's eyes widened. "Stop that." She giggled as she swatted my hands away. "You know what I'm talking about."

"I know, I know. I'm just joking with you. I'm sorry, and I'm sure your *diorama*," I emphasized the word, "is very pretty."

I couldn't decide whether or not to bring up the boo-boo. I looked at Mollie's little face and just couldn't stand to see her cry by revealing that Mom's boo-boo wasn't so little after all. The last thing Mollie needed was to have big puffy brown eyes in the morning.

I said good night to Mollie and kissed her on the head before I went back to my room.

"Good night, Mom and Dad." I opened their door an inch.

"Love you," they called after me.

When I was finally in bed, I put my face into my pillow and stared at the dancing colors, the only thing that could distract me from the loneliness I felt at the moment. Mollie was always jealous of how big my room was. She said that I didn't need such a big room because I was so small. She was wrong.

Lying in bed that night I felt squished. There just wasn't enough room for the two of us: my big fat secret and me.

CHAPTER 7

I decided I'd keep Mom's secret from my siblings. It would be her job to tell them. I had to deal with something way worse. My friends.

I didn't want to tell any of them, yet I never knew what would come out of my Big Mouth. It was mostly because I didn't know what to say but also because I didn't want my friends to treat me differently.

I tried to forget about Mom and focused on spelling, fractions, and the speed of light. Mr. Dawn also told me I had to turn in a drawing by the end of the day to make up for the assignment I'd missed that day I skipped class, so I needed to find time to do that.

By recess, I was in desperate need of fresh air. When the bell rang, I happily took my package of *Chips Ahoy!* Mom packed and followed my friends to the playground.

We went to our usual spot—the bridge that connected the end of the jungle gym with the yellow twisty slide, to the side with the straight boring slide. We didn't care that we blocked the entire walkway because that's where the cool kids always sat.

Today it was just Hailey and me on the bridge. The rest of our friends were in the principal's office because they weren't following the school's dress code. We were happy to hang out alone.

Hailey and I were best friends. This meant we *had* to get all the same school supplies, be in the same classes, and sit next to each other during every subject. And even though we didn't have the same backpack, we approved each other's choices before buying them. We tried to have long phone conversations like adults, but most of the time one of us fell asleep before we even reached the one-hour mark.

"What do you think you're going to get for Hanukkah?" Hailey asked once we sat down.

Hanukkah was one of my favorite parts of being Jewish. We celebrated for eight days, and on one of the nights our entire family got together to exchange gifts, eat *latkes*, and light the menorah together. Mom's mom, my Bobby, made the best potato pancakes, and my mouth watered at the thought of eating them again in almost two weeks.

"I don't know."

And I was telling the truth. I didn't know. Mom was having surgery right before the holiday, which meant a lot of things would change. Would we be having Hanukkah? Who would put together our Hanukkah party? Who would buy our presents? In the past, it was always Mom.

"What does that mean?" Hailey asked as a little first grader tried to get past us on the bridge. She ended up tripping on Hailey's foot.

"I just don't know where I will be." I shrugged and looked at the sky, at anything other than Hailey's face. I stuffed a cookie in my mouth and concentrated on chewing, hoping the cookie would block the truth that was dying to come out.

"Won't you be with your family?"

My face fell. I swallowed.

"Ari, what's wrong?"

At that moment, a girl jumped on the bridge sending Hailey and me flying on our butts and my cookie out of my hands. And if it weren't for what I was about to say, I would have burst out laughing.

Once the bridge was stable, I said, "I can't tell you . . . you're going to laugh." I was taught that *breast* was a bathroom word, and I couldn't bring myself to say it in front of Hailey.

"I swear I won't laugh. What is it?"

"My mom is having surgery. She has *breast* cancer. I don't think she'll be able to cook or buy presents or any of that normal stuff. I don't think we'll be having much of a holiday at all," I blurted.

Hailey paled. She didn't know what to say, which was exactly what I had feared. What was a fifth grader supposed to say to that? This was heavy stuff. I already felt like I was carrying the weight of the world on my shoulders.

When she didn't say anything right away I assumed she was just deciding how to digest what I had told her. I mean, they didn't teach kids how to deal with real-world drama in elementary school, so this topic was pretty much out of any fifth grader's comfort zone. But Hailey shocked me by proving me wrong—she knew exactly what to do.

She hugged me and whispered, "Everything is going to be okay. If you need me, I'm here."

I hugged her back, tight. That was why I picked her as my best friend. She knew what to say and how to say it.

"Thanks, Hailey," I said into her ear. "Just don't tell anybody." Another girl tried to get past Hailey and me, but she gave up once she saw we weren't breaking apart anytime soon. Hailey nodded. She wouldn't tell anyone. Hailey knowing was one thing, but having the entire grade know scared me. I decided this breast cancer thing would be a breeze. Maybe I would even tell Sam and Mollie and they would see that it was going to be okay just like Hailey had. And between my family and Hailey, I would have all the support I needed.

I told Hailey I had to catch up on some homework before class started again. I went back to my classroom and sat at my desk. I ripped out a piece of fresh white paper and stared at it for a minute.

My favorite place was supposed to be somewhere where I felt safe, which was why the obvious answer was Mom. She was always there for me, helping me and doing things for me that I couldn't possibly take care of myself.

But Mom couldn't always protect me. She wasn't going to be strong enough after the surgery and I wouldn't let her do anything for me if that meant she would get sick again. I had to learn how to take care of myself a little bit and that meant letting other people in to help me, like Hailey.

I took a pink crayon and drew my new favorite place—somewhere I felt brave without Mom. The bridge.

CHAPTER 8

"Spit!" Raquel yelled so loud my ears hurt.

As all my friends were sitting in the classroom waiting for our afternoon teacher to come in, we played our favorite card game in the entire world: Spit. We transformed the game of Spit from something grandparents played because they didn't know how to work an iPhone into a huge tournament that, if you were to lose, your entire life could change. To be honest, it wasn't that serious, but our class did not take any game of Spit lightly, ever.

We played Spit during any free time we had, between class periods, during recess, and even during lunch. But we also loved the school's yummy food, so we always made sure we had enough time to eat during lunchtime, too.

This particular morning my friends and I wanted to try something new. You see, Zoe and Raquel were the Spit Masters of our class. They yelled the loudest, put the cards down the fastest, and have been the reigning champions of Class 5S for the past year. Now they wanted to see who was best once and for all. And because this was a big deal, we decided to make things interesting and play the regular game of Spit, but with a twist.

We came up with these rules:

1. Winner can partner up with the smartest girl in class for the next assignment

2. Loser has to tell Dylan Weinstein—the cutest boy in our grade—that she likes him
   2a. Rule #2 can be done on the school portal to save some embarrassment
3. If either participant cheats, they are not allowed to play Spit in Class 5S ever again

Our teachers communicated with us through an online portal. They sent us homework and assignments and made sure we received them. Since each of us had a personal screen name, no one was able to say they did not have access to an assignment as an excuse for not turning it in to the teacher on time. This was also the administration's evil way of keeping us in the loop on Snow Days and while on vacation.

The portal's primary purpose was for us to communicate with our teachers, but since many of us didn't have a cell phone yet, we often sat online chatting about homework or whatever television show was airing that night. The best part was that teachers did not have any access to our messages. There was one catch: since there are so many students in our school, you had to know the screen name of the student you were messaging before sending a direct message. One time Hailey spelled my screen name wrong and ended up messaging an eighth grader! She was lucky that eighth graders don't use the portal because that's even more embarrassing than sending a direct message to a boy like Dylan.

Anyway, once the rules were written on a piece of paper and signed by both players, we began the tournament. Raquel and Zoe sat on the floor across from one another, each with half a deck of cards in their hands. They anxiously stared at their cards and leaned forward on their knees as if they were runners in a race.

The entire class crowded around Raquel and Zoe in a circle, surrounding the players, on the colorful checkered floor. Excitement filled the air. Everyone was ready to see who would finally be named Spit Champion for good.

"Is everyone ready?" Raquel said as she looked around the class.

Class 5S nodded in unison.

"Alright," she said, "Hailey, take it from here."

Hailey didn't love to play the game of Spit so she took on the role of Announcer. To be honest, it fit her dramatic personality *very* well.

"Class 5S, let me hear you scream!" Hailey stood up in between the two girls and raised her hands above her head. "But not too loud because we don't want Principal Hale to come in here." She quickly added.

We all did the silent cheer, which consisted of doing jazz fingers above our heads and opening our mouths wide like we were yelling.

"Raquel and Zoe," she squatted down to their level and looked at both of them as she spoke, "I want a smooth match from the both of you. You can begin on three."

The entire class chanted together, "One, two . . ."

"Three," Hailey said.

And the game began.

The game went on for a while. There was no clear winner for the entire first half. After about four rounds, Zoe accidentally hit the larger pile and Raquel easily slipped into the lead. Raquel had the game in the bag after that.

Five minutes before recess was officially over, Raquel slammed an ace of spades on top of the two and smacked the ground next to the tall pile of cards. She yelled the final, "Spit!" and won the game.

The crowd started to disperse as Hailey raised Raquel's arm in the air and announced, "Give a round of applause to our new class champion! Shake hands girls."

Raquel's face was glowing as she accepted "congratulations" from all the girls around her. Zoe, on the other hand, looked like she was going to cry.

"Are you kidding me?" Zoe covered her eyes with her hands. "You guys, I can't talk to Dylan. I've never spoken to him in my life."

And of course, Eva added, "I have his screen name. I can give it to you."

"No one asked you." Hailey was annoyed and gave me a she's-so-annoying look. I shot back a can-she-just-go-back-to-the-boys'-side-of-the-school look.

Eva always hung out on the boys' side of the school. And she always came back with some crazy story that was never as interesting as she tried to make it seem. One time she snuck to the boys' side of the school during one of her bathroom breaks. We're not allowed to go to their side of the school ever. But Eva did not get caught. She came back from her bathroom break so happy you would think she'd won a million dollars in the lottery.

She got the entire class to be quiet and told us the big news: we would never have to fill out our vocabulary books again because she had already gotten a filled-out one from one of the boys. Eva expected Class 5S to get excited about that, except we didn't. Why would a class of smart girls need to copy vocabulary from the boys? Then she got angry and ran out of class.

So if Eva gave Zoe Dylan's screen name it would just be another time that Eva made everything about her. But I wasn't going to let that happen. Not this time. And then it hit me. I realized I had something no one else had—a twin brother.

Sam knew Dylan and could help Zoe talk to him, and no one would need to ask Eva for help. Maybe this time *I* would be the one with the cool story about a boy, and Eva would just sit on the side with her strange hairstyle and cry. Maybe she wouldn't cry, but I bet she would be really mad.

"Zoe, my brother can give you Dylan's screen name." I smiled at her, trying my best to ignore Eva's evil glare.

"I can give it to her too," Eva whined, clearly wanting to fight over this.

A little voice inside of me begged me to stop what I was about to do and wondered why I cared so much. I could've stayed out of the whole mess entirely. Maybe I thought that it was an opportunity for me to forget about Mom or maybe I just needed to control something in my life since everything at home was about to explode.

"Maybe I can even do it at your house from Sam's portal so it doesn't look as weird." Zoe looked at Raquel and asked, "Is that allowed under the rules?"

The Spit Tournament was not a joke. We had rules. Raquel announced to the class: "Does everyone think that Zoe talking to Dylan about liking him is embarrassing enough that she can do it from Sam's portal instead of her own? Raise your hand if you think yes."

And we all raised our hands. Zoe did a little dance of joy and hugged me. She smiled so big you would think *she* won the lottery.

"I'll come over tonight, and we'll do it?" Zoe asked.

"You got it."

Hailey looked at me with a smile, and I knew what she was thinking. I mouthed, "Yes. You're coming, too."

It dawned on me that inviting friends to come over might not have been the best idea. My house wasn't very welcoming with everything going on—someone was either crying or talking about which doctor Mom should call first. But I couldn't let Mom's breast cancer get in the way of helping Zoe. And I wasn't going to tell Zoe the reason why she couldn't come over. Cancer wasn't supposed to take over *my* life, even though everywhere I turned I could see it spreading.

CHAPTER 9

"Arianna, Hailey's here," Mom called.

I quickly got up from the kitchen table and raced to the door, scared of what Hailey might say to Mom. Would she say anything to her about being sick? Do you say, "feel better" to someone with cancer? I didn't know because I never knew anyone who was sick, especially with cancer. The universe was *always* teaching me something new.

"Hi, Hailey," I said. Then I looked at Mom standing in the doorway. "Zoe is coming also. I hope that's okay?"

Since I didn't ask Mom if it was okay to have people over on a school night, I decided to ask her as one of my guests stood in the doorway. It was better late than never, and she wasn't going to slam the door in Hailey's face. That would be rude.

"Of course, but it's a school night, so don't stay up too late. Are you guys doing a project together or something?" I usually always told Mom when I had something due for school, so she must have thought it was weird I hadn't mentioned anything beforehand.

Hailey and I looked at each other and said at the same time, "Something like that." We *were* working on a project, but Mom didn't have to know if it was for school or not.

"All right. Not too late, girls," Mom said. Then she went back to the dining room table where she was explaining the difference between the words "there" and "their" to Mollie.

"Thanks, Mrs. Goodman." Hailey said to Mom and continued in the sweetest voice, "It's so nice of you to have us tonight when you didn't even know that I was coming."

Okay, Hailey was pushing it. She never spoke to Mom in such a sweet voice. This was exactly why I didn't want people to know Mom had breast cancer. At first, I had thought my friends would treat me differently, but instead, they were treating Mom differently. I guess she needed some special treatment. After all, The Evil Breast Cancer Disease was inside her. I let Hailey's over-the-top niceness go.

Mom said over my sister's shoulder, "It's no problem, Hailey." Then she continued with Mollie.

I turned to Hailey. "So, are you always going to be this nice to my mom?"

Hailey laughed as she ran up the stairs to my room. I could tell she was nervous after talking to her, but she was being strong for me.

"All right, what's step one to our mission?" I asked Hailey as I sat on the floor in my room. I hated sitting on the floor, but I never sat on my clean bed when I was in my school clothes.

Hailey took a seat on my white desk. She moved all my textbooks over to one side so she could put her smelly feet up. I made a note in my head to clean that spot after she left. "We need to help Zoe talk to Dylan without making a fool of herself."

"And how are we going to do that if we have never spoken to Dylan?" I was completely lost and honestly afraid that all of this would eventually lead me to have to talk to Dylan.

"First we have to get Sam on board. Then we can get Zoe to talk to Dylan," Hailey explained.

"Then all we have to do is print out the conversation to show our friends that Zoe spoke to him. That's what Raquel told me we should do for it to be official," I reminded Hailey. I got up and smacked her feet off my desk. They'd been perched up there long enough.

She giggled. "Perfect. So tonight we'll complete Mission Z. Z for Zoe." Hailey clapped her hands and ran toward Sam's room down the hall. She looked back at me before turning the gold doorknob and said, "Well, here goes nothing." Shrugging, she pushed Sam's door open.

And there he was. Sam was fast asleep in front of his laptop that was playing old videos of *I Love Lucy*. I couldn't even see his body because he was covered in a million wrappers of Laffy Taffys. He was always eating.

"So this," I pointed to my sleeping brother, "is going to interfere with Mission Z."

Hailey whispered, "Well, do you have any ideas?"

"Hmmm." I tapped my finger to my temple before saying, "You know I always have ideas." And with that, I jumped on Sam and yelled, "I NEED HELP WITH MY MATH HOMEWORK!"

I still didn't know how that worked because Sam had always been an extremely heavy sleeper. This time Sam magically woke up. I guess it was the pain he felt when I punched him in the back or the pressure from my knee in his shoulder that made him jump up so quickly. Maybe it was the mention of *math* that woke him up.

He seemed very confused after he opened his eyes. They were bright red, like how your eyes look after swimming for a lot of hours. And he just stared at Hailey and me like he didn't know what was going on or what was about to happen.

"Wh-what are you doing in here?" he said while rubbing his eyes again.

"We need you to help us with something really important but you have to promise," I narrowed my eyes. "Sam, you have to promise not to tell anyone." I squinted my eyes, tightened my jaw, and flared my noes. It was the most serious face I could make. He must have understood because he brushed off all the millions of wrappers and sat upright in bed.

"Sure. What's up?" He yawned. I mean, how tired could he be? It was like seven thirty at night, he was eating candy, and it looked like he had only watched fifteen minutes of his TV show.

But right when I was about to explain the situation Mom yelled, "Arianna! Hailey! Come down. Zoe's here!"

I froze, looking from Sam to Hailey. Ready or not, Mission Z was officially in motion.

CHAPTER 10

I could tell Sam was confused. He was very distracted, bopping up and down on his bed and fidgeting with his hands. I hoped it was the candy giving him a sugar rush and there was nothing wrong with his brain. We had explained the plan to him, and even though people called him the smarter twin, he couldn't seem to understand Mission Z.

"Let me get this straight." He yawned again. "You want to message Dylan that you like him, but you don't really like him? And no one can know that you don't really like him?" He raised one of his eyebrows like he always did when he was concentrating. "Then why do you want to tell him that you like him in the first place?"

Hailey and I looked at each other. We were exhausted, and Zoe was getting antsy. I let Hailey explain it to him this time. "See, that's the part that we *can't* tell you." She was leaning against his desk; her hands were pressed against her cheeks and she did not look happy. She was ready to give in and tell Sam about our bet, but I wasn't going to break that easily, especially if it meant giving Eva any satisfaction.

I said, "No. Raquel said that we can't tell anyone, and Sam counts as an 'anyone.' I don't get why we are even explaining this to him."

"Fine." Hailey threw her hands in the air. "Let's do this already. I'm getting nervous."

Sam just stared at us like we were animals in a cage and mumbled, "I just don't get girls sometimes." I ignored him.

"*You're* getting nervous," Zoe blurted. "I have never talked to the kid in my life. Only Eva has! He's not even going to know who I am."

She was sitting on the corner of Sam's couch curled up like a little girl who was afraid of her mom. I bet she wondered what would've happened if she had just yelled "Spit" a little louder and faster.

"Okay, do whatever you want." He gave in. As if on cue, he went to his desk, turned his computer on, and signed into his account.

"But what if Dylan isn't online?" Zoe asked. She seemed excited about that.

"A boy like Dylan is always online," Hailey said as she sat down on the desk next to the computer. Didn't she ever want to sit on a chair?

"What in the world is that supposed to mean?" Sam shook his head. "Whatever. Just call me when you're done. I'm going to watch TV." And Sam left us alone in his room with his account open, with every boy our age's screen name out there for us to take.

We huddled around the computer. Zoe and I shared the chair that was directly in front of the screen. "Ready?"

"No!" She turned to face me, her face bright red. "Can't we just say that I did it and not do it? Does this bet really matter? It was a game of Spit."

"It's not just a game," I said under my breath.

Hailey jumped off the desk and yelled at Zoe, "We have to do it now. If we don't, Eva will make fun of you for the rest of the year. Do you understand how long a year is? Message him, Zoe! He's just a boy."

"He's not *just* a boy! He's Dylan." She got up and circled the room.

And that's when it hit me—it was as obvious as Sam's sugar addiction: Zoe liked Dylan. I had never known anyone my age with a crush on a boy before. This made complete sense though. She really didn't want to do it because she liked him. If she didn't like him, she would have done it already and acted like it was all a big joke. But she was seriously about to cry, and there was only one possible explanation, which was that Zoe liked Dylan.

I looked at Hailey, who was steaming mad. She didn't see what I saw: Zoe liked Dylan!

I had to stop this from happening. I'd be horrified if I had to tell a boy I actually liked that I liked him, even if it was a joke.

"You know what, Zoe?" I said as I twisted Sam's chair around to face my two friends who were freaking out. "I think we should do this a different night. We can tell everyone that we did it, and then just say my printer was broken. It's fine. There will be another Spit game tomorrow, and everyone will forget about this."

"But . . . the bet. We can't." Zoe was shocked I had given in.

"Exactly, Ari, THE BET! We made a deal, and we can't break it." Hailey looked mad, but I wasn't giving in. I blocked the computer with my body and said, "I'm signing out."

"Ugh." Hailey stomped out of Sam's room.

Zoe said, "Thank you." And then she walked to the bathroom in the hallway. She looked like she was about to burst into tears, but not because she was sad. She looked really happy.

Once they were both gone, I slumped down in the chair. I was glad it was over. I was about to sign off Sam's account and go and see if Hailey was still steaming mad when I realized what was right in front of me. I was logged into Sam's account, and I could make a status on his account that every boy and girl he had ever messaged with could see. My body buzzed with excitement as I scrolled through his messages. He seemed to have messaged everyone in the fifth grade. I thought about not doing it for a second, but I quickly shook that thought away. I had nothing to lose.

I cleared away his status that read: *Available*. I wrote: *Eva likes Mason Silverman*. Then I signed off and ran to my room as quickly as if I had just escaped prison. I was too excited.

I told Zoe and Hailey what I had done, and we laughed so hard that I thought my appendix was going to explode. I think it made them forget about what had happened earlier.

"Mason Silverman?" Hailey's face beamed. "He's like the cutest boy in the eighth grade. I wonder what Eva's going to do when she sees that."

"I bet she'll think that all of the eighth-grade boys sit around and talk about her all night." Zoe was smiling, but probably because we finally stopped talking about Mission Z.

"Or she'll get really mad at Sam." Hailey looked at me.

"Well, I hadn't thought of that." My plan very well may end up backfiring. I shut my eyes and put my hand to my forehead. "Sam is going to kill me."

I got up from the floor and paced my room trying to assess the situation. I signed out from his account already, so I had no way of deleting the status. I had no other option other than confronting Sam. Sam was going to be so mad that I messed with his account. I needed my friends to leave before they saw *his* explosion.

"Wait, do you think Eva is going to find out who made the status?" Zoe asked, ignoring my sudden crisis of conscience.

"You need to stop being so afraid of everything, Zoe," Hailey snapped at her. I quickly shot Hailey a look, trying to telepathically tell her to be nicer to Zoe.

I put my hair up in a ponytail, then changed my mind about it and let my hair back down. I sat at my desk and outlined the picture on the cover of my math textbook. If my friends saw that I was getting restless maybe they would get the hint that I wanted—needed—them to leave.

"Either way, Eva's going to freak out tomorrow. Mission Z was not completed," Hailey said as she put her jacket on. In my mind, I patted myself on the back. They had gotten the hint and both called their moms to pick them up.

"But we're going to make our entire grade think that Eva likes Mason." Zoe squealed as we went downstairs to wait for their moms. Then she stopped. "Wait, isn't that sort of mean?"

I checked to see if Sam was still watching TV in the living room and hadn't gone back up to his room yet. Out of the corner of my eye, I saw him staring at the screen. He didn't look like he was going anywhere soon.

"I bet when Mason finds out that she likes him he asks her out. Who wouldn't be happy to go out with Eva? She's so pretty." Zoe sighed. "All this for nothing."

Seeming to ignore Zoe, Hailey chimed in, "You're right, Zoe, every boy wants to go out with the Leaning Tower of Eva." Hailey took the front pieces of her hair and made them into a poof like Eva and the poof-girls' hair.

I couldn't help from laughing and neither could Zoe.

Hailey bent down and looked at the mirror across from my stairs. She yelled, "Ahhh," and she pointed to it. "That girl's hair is quite scary." Quickly, she put it up into a pony. "Now *that* looks much better," she said as she smoothed down the top pieces with her hands.

Zoe and I were hysterically laughing at Hailey's show. Hailey was curtseying and patting herself on the back as she complimented herself,

"I'm here all night! Just call me the Hair Goddess and follow me on Instagram. Yes, I know… I'm adorable."

But once I was cured of the giggles I turned to Hailey and spoke very seriously. "Ok, stop making fun," She frowned, and Zoe stuck her tongue out at her. Ignoring their banter, I continued, "Guys, we must forget about this. We can't bring too much attention to the status tomorrow because then people will ask us about Zoe, who didn't complete the bet," I reminded them.

I didn't know which topic was better to talk about, the fact we hadn't completed the mission, or the fact I was about to run upstairs and delete the status that had suddenly changed the mood.

"Wait. Seriously. . . Then what should we tell everyone tomorrow?" Zoe asked.

Through the window, I saw two cars waiting, so I said, "We're just going to pretend that nothing happened. Because nothing did happen." I faked a smile as I opened the door and waved goodbye.

Hailey turned to me while waving. "Yeah. It's like we were never even here."

I closed the door before either of them could see I was just as worried as they were. I leaned my back against the brown door and sighed. After a moment of relaxation, I got back to business.

"Sam," I yelled from the foyer. He didn't answer because he was too distracted by the TV. I walked to the living room. "Sam!" I nudged his shoulder.

"Ari, you have got to stop yelling my name. What do you need now?" He raised his eyebrows and crossed his arms.

"I need to sign back on to your account," I asked hesitantly.

"Do I even want to know why?"

"It would be so nice if you didn't ask."

"Fine. But only because I need to watch the end of this before Mom makes me go to sleep." He got up from the couch leaving an imprint from where he'd been sitting.

I rolled my eyes before following him upstairs. Sam took two steps at a time and raced to his room, closing the door in my face before I had a chance to enter.

"Why did you do that?" I opened the door and stood over him.

"Do what?" His eyes were twinkling with mischief. Older brothers got so much satisfaction by making their younger sisters miserable. And he was only older by five minutes.

"Whatever." I let the door-slam-in-the-face go. I just needed to delete the status, like five minutes ago. "Can you just sign back into your account?"

"Done." Sam signed back in and got up from the chair. "I'm going back downstairs. Are you going to be able to stay signed in this time or do you need a babysitter?"

"Oh, be quiet." I stuck my tongue out at him as he closed the door. Then called, "Thank you!"

Quickly, I deleted the status. I leaned back in Sam's chair and let out a deep breath. I didn't know what the next day was going to bring. Mission Z was incomplete and although Mission Delete Embarrassing Status was a success, the damage was already done. Someone was bound to have seen the status in the past half hour. I just hoped with all my might that it wasn't Eva.

CHAPTER 11

The next day started strangely.

First, when I got on the bus, Hannah gave me the window seat. The window seat had always been her seat since the first grade. We never actually wrote our names, but it was an unspoken agreement between us that I *never* broke, even though I wished I could look out the window during the bus ride instead of the ugly black tape on the back of the seat in front of me.

Then in school, not one person mentioned the bet. Not even Zoe or Hailey, who were freaking out about it the night before. And luckily, no one mentioned the fact there was a mysterious status on Sam's account last night, which made me feel extra relieved.

And if that didn't seem weird enough, during lunch when I was eating the toasted bagel with cheese and tomato Mom packed me, I realized someone was staring at me. I was sitting at the end of the table alone because Hailey had forgotten her lunch upstairs, so I thought maybe it was because I was alone. Still, I could feel her eyes burning into the back of my neck.

Then it got even weirder. I got up to throw out my empty brown paper lunch bag when a girl from the other fifth-grade class came over to me and asked, "Hey Ari, I just wanted to know if you are OK and let you know I am here if you need anything." To make matters worse, she frowned at me and gave me a sympathetic pat on my forearm.

My eyes widened and I quickly walked away from her. Did I not *look* okay? I thought I looked cute. Besides the usual blue skirt and white collared shirt that was our school's dress code, I put a pink clip in my hair to tame my curls. And I thought they were tame.

Then things became chaotic. One by one, girls came over to my spot at the lunch table, telling me they were there for me, and I could sleep over if I wanted to, and I could copy their notes when I missed class. I never thought I had that many friends and I never spoke to that many girls during lunch in my life.

It was only after my friend Nikki said, "Is your mom feeling okay?" that I understood the situation. Suddenly the room began to spin around me.

Everyone knew that Mom was sick.

Immediately the world crashed down around me. I looked at Nikki and said, "Wait . . . who told you?"

"I . . . I don't know what you're talking about," she answered and walked away.

Word that my mother had breast cancer got around my entire grade fast. *Everyone* knew, and I wanted to know who told them. But no one was going to let me in on the big secret, so I left.

I ran up to my classroom where I could be alone. I sat down at my desk and put my head on the cold tabletop. I didn't start crying right away because for once I had nothing real to cry about. The truth was, there was nothing I could do now that everyone knew. The reason I was so upset was that there was only one possible person who could have told everyone: Hailey. And the idea of her breaking our promise made me sad, sick, and tired all at the same time. I just sat and stared at the multi-colored floor and thought about all the reasons I hated Hailey.

Then I felt a hand on my back. My stomach did that weird floppy thing that told me I was afraid and then I looked up. It was Hailey.

"Did you tell people about my mom, Hailey?" I asked. I was trying not to burst into tears when I looked at her.

The happy smile on her face transformed into a frown. "Me? I promised you that I would never tell anyone. I would *never* do that to you, Ari." She knelt by me so she could look at my face. I had to believe her. I needed her more than ever.

Still, it didn't make sense how suddenly everyone knew about Mom. I'd only told one person. I might as well have screamed over a megaphone, "My mom has breast cancer. Pity me now!" But *I* didn't, so then *who* did?

"Do you know who did?" I put my hand through my hair, ruining the perfect placement of my cute pink clip.

"Forget that. Are you okay?" She sat down at her desk.

"Not really," I said shaking my head.

She took a deep breath. "I know it's hard, but this is better. You don't want to be keeping such a big secret all to yourself. We can all help you." When I didn't answer right away she added, "Come on, secrets are no fun unless you share them with everyone."

I giggled. "I know you're right, Hailey. I just hated being stared at like...," I couldn't find the right word so I settled with, "I'm different . . . And I was sitting all alone. Wait, what took you so long?"

She giggled, "I couldn't find my lunch, and then I realized that I left it on the bus." I couldn't help but laugh. She always left something on the bus. One time she went through a whole day of school without noticing she had left her backpack on the bus. After school, her mom had to call the bus company to track down a hot-pink Minnie Mouse backpack.

"Can we stay up here until class starts?" I sat up straight and rubbed my eyes.

"Sure," Hailey said as she took something out of her bag. She held up a deck of cards. "Want to play Spit?" My eyes widened in shock.

"You're joking?" But she shook her head. "You better not make me message Dylan if I lose."

At that moment Eva came into the classroom. She was hiding her face with a tissue and I would bet a million dollars that she had been crying. The minute she saw us she looked like a deer in headlights—she was caught. She quickly crumpled the tissue in her hands.

Sitting down at her desk, Eva flipped her hair and crossed her legs. I swear I even heard her sniffle but I had a feeling she didn't want to talk about it. "Haven't you played enough card games yet?"

Hailey cupped her mouth with her hand so Eva couldn't see and whispered, "I'll take this one." Then she stared Eva straight in the eyes and lied, "We spoke to Dylan last night. The bet is over, Eva."

Even though we were lying to Eva for the sake of Zoe, it felt wrong. I hated keeping secrets and keeping track of the lies we had to tell to keep our secrets safe were just not worth it. I could tell we were making a mess the minute Eva said, "I'll need some proof."

"This is not a police station and you're *not* part of the FBI." Hailey did not hesitate and I was impressed. "I told you we did it. And now it's over."

"Whatever," She turned around and I think she wiped her eyes on the crumpled tissue. "I'm so over messaging on that portal anyways. Haven't you guys heard of DMing on Instagram?" And with that, she got up to leave.

"Wait," I finally spoke. My voice sounded a little raspy because I'd been crying.

"So now you're speaking, Ari?" Eva turned around and crossed her arms.

I ignored the venom in her comment. "Are you okay?" I felt Hailey's glare on my back and suddenly became nervous. My voice cracked when I spoke. "I mean, um, you looked, well, sort of sad."

Eva's expression seemed to change from anger to shock and back to anger. "What makes you think that I'm upset? I'm just going to meet Mason. Have you heard of him? I bet you haven't. He's in eighth grade, which is on the *other* side of the school. I heard that both of you don't go there too often." Then she clicked her heels together and started out the door. But she wasn't finished. She poked her head back in and looked straight at me while she sang the words, "Oh, Arianna, I hope your mom's feeling better. I heard she's sick." And with that, she flipped her hair and left.

Hailey took a seat at her desk and turned to me. Her eyes were blinking in disbelief. "I have no words right now."

"Did she just say that?" I pointed to where Eva had been standing wondering if our encounter had been a dream.

"Is she really meeting Mason?" Hailey asked combing a hand through her hair.

"I could've sworn she was crying. I just wanted to know if she was okay and then she had to bring my mom into it. That was so mean." I put my left cheek on my desk so I was facing Hailey.

"Ari, do not let Eva get to you," she said to try to make me feel better. Then to try to make herself feel better she continued, "I bet she's making up that story about Mason. And how does she even know that we don't go to the boys' side of the school?" I knew it bothered her that Eva talked to boys more than she did. "And she seemed like she felt a little sorry for you about your—"

"Ugh." I lifted my head a little bit too quickly and I saw tiny stars in the corner of my vision. I rubbed my eyes and said, "That's exactly what I don't want."

"Fine. Then we won't talk about your mom anymore. Done." Hailey said while slamming her hands on the desk like a judge does with his hammer after closing a case.

"We're so lucky Eva believed us. Zoe owes us one." I slumped in my chair and let myself relax. All of this was too much for one day and talking about failed Mission Z was a good enough topic change. But then it hit me and I propped up in my seat. "Wait, why do you think she was crying?"

Hailey shrugged.

"Do you think she found out about the status?"

She shrugged again. She seemed to be done with talking about *everything* at the moment, not just Mom.

"I'm serious."

"As long as she doesn't know it was us we're in the clear, Ari. Enjoy it."

I slumped back in my chair and waited for class to start. I couldn't just enjoy it. I had a strong sense that Eva was upset because of me, and I didn't even dare to say sorry.

CHAPTER 12

I should have been happy when I got home. Zoe had been thrilled when Raquel announced to the class that her debt to the bet had been paid and it was all because of Hailey and me. But I came home frustrated with myself for even feeling sorry for Eva and angry with Mom that she had cancer.

"Mom, I'm home!" I yelled as loud as I could.

I guess she heard how angry I was because she ran to meet me by the front door. "Is everything okay, sweetie?"

"I told Hailey that you would need surgery and why you would need it. She told me that she didn't tell anyone, but for some reason, everyone in school knows. I didn't want everyone to know, Mom! I don't want them to treat me differently." I began to cry. Crying was becoming a habit, and I secretly hated myself for becoming a sensitive tween.

Mom's eyes widened and she put one hand on her forehead and the other on my shoulder. "This is my fault. I forgot to tell you that I spoke to the social worker at school, and she agreed it would be beneficial for you if you spoke to her once in a while. I also told some of your friends' moms, and I guess they told their kids. I had no idea. I am so sorry," she said and hugged me.

"You think I need to see a social worker? Are you kidding, Mom? I am a kid. With a mother. Who has cancer! I need *you*, Mom." I unwrapped myself from her grip and stomped around the foyer screaming, instantly proving to myself right then and there that crying was a habit. I had officially transformed into a self-absorbed drama queen.

When I felt like I had done enough stomping and my tantrum was coming to an end, I ran upstairs to my room. I thought I'd feel better crying on my bed instead of on the hard floor. And I hoped Mom would follow me, of course.

But what I saw when I first walked into my room did *not* make me feel better, and I screamed at the top of my lungs.

I wasn't normally a scaredy-cat. I was one of those girls who always went with the Scary Group at amusement parks, and I have watched scary movies like *The Gooneys* since I was eight. But what was on my computer, in my little pink room, was way scarier than any rollercoaster or movie I ever experienced.

My computer screen was filled with pictures of naked women with deformed boobs. I didn't get a chance to see the pictures clearly because I started crying again, but what I saw *was* horrifying. There were at least twenty women who weren't wearing anything over the top part of their bodies. The pictures showed the area in between the waist and the neck, giving me a perfect view of their chest. Well, I guess that was the point. But their boobs looked terrible. Each had large pink scars running from one side to the other. It looked like it was right out of a horror movie. It looked like the work of The Evil Breast Cancer Disease.

Mom was right behind me when I yelled so she got to see the entire show, but Dad came running into my room. He was out of breath. "What's wrong?" he asked. "I thought you saw a mouse again."

One time, my family came home from vacation only to find a dead mouse under the radiator in Mollie's room. It was funny because the mouse was dead and in my neat freak sister's room. She had the biggest temper tantrum in the entire universe and refused to sleep in her room until her carpet was professionally cleaned.

"This is worse than the time with the mouse." I stomped my feet like a baby and sat on my bed. "What are those pictures? And what are they doing on *my* computer?" I pointed to them to prove my point.

Once Dad realized what was on the screen, he knew he had done something wrong. He threw his hands up to his head in disbelief and sat down beside me on my bed. "It's my fault, sweetie. I forgot to log off your computer." He looked sorry for me that I had to see those pictures. He knew how hard this was for me.

The entire time Mom was silent, though. She just sat on the other side of me and rubbed my back. Finally, after what seemed like a lifetime of silence, she spoke. "Your father and I were just researching about my boo-boo. We want to find the best way the doctors can get rid of the cancer for good." She sounded calm, but I could tell from the scared look in her eyes that she was afraid of the women in the pictures also. She spoke extremely slowly as if she was also explaining the information to herself. "I had to decide if I want to get rid of just the cancer that is only in one of my breasts or to get rid of both my breasts so that I never have to worry about getting breast cancer again." She looked at my Dad, who gave her a reassuring nod. "With your Dad and our doctors, I decided that I want to take both of my breasts off so that we never have to go through this again. It is called a double mastectomy. Does this make sense to you, Ari?"

"So your boobs are going to look like *those*?" I ignored her question, looking at the naked women on the screen again.

Mom flinched, making the bed creak. I suddenly realized that I was overreacting and this would affect my mother more than me. After all, it wasn't my body.

"You know, you don't need to make me feel bad. I know that you're scared, Arianna, but I am trying to explain to you the types of decisions we have to make right now. I know this is hard for you, but I promise everything is going to be okay. If I didn't believe that for sure, then I wouldn't make you a promise like this." She looked straight at the screen as she spoke. Then she looked at Dad who took a seat at my desk chair, trying to block the computer.

"Listen to Mommy, everything's going to be just fine," Dad said.

And he was not the optimist. In fact, Dad was the complete opposite. He worried about every little thing possible. He worried about work and bills. Most of all, he worried about Mom.

Sometimes when you're quiet, you can hear Dad yell out Mom's name throughout the day. He said that it's because when he's not with Mom, he misses her so much he just must yell out her name. Some people would think it's romantic, but my family and I think it's creepy.

I guess I would rather have Dad whispering Mom's name out to the world over anything else. He adored her and would do anything for her. And if *he* thought everything was going to be okay, then it would be.

"I think that's smart of you, Mom. To, um, get rid of them for good. I don't ever want to see you sick again." I wrapped my arm around her waist and leaned against her. "So when's the surgery?"

"Three days," Dad said. His tone sounded happy, but the worried look in his eyes gave him away.

"Great." Mom put her hand on top of mine as if to say again, "everything's going to be fine."

SURGERY

CHAPTER 13

My family had never been very optimistic. Whenever we had a sports game, a test, or any type of deadline, we were always negative. We thought the worst would come, and though I would like to tell you the opposite, the worst showed up.

Like at my brother's hockey game. My entire family went to his school and sat in the hot, smelly gym to see Sam play and cheer him on. Sam wasn't playing very well on Monday night, and his team was losing. And Sam's team was pretty good, and they were playing a pretty bad team, so everyone in the crowd was extra annoyed to be there and very disappointed.

Mom and I walked in a little late, and once she saw the score, she stopped and said, "I *cannot* be here. I'm a bad luck charm." She started to turn around, but Dad had seen her walk in and was already wrapping his arm around her and pushing her toward the bleachers.

He whispered in her ear, "You are here for Sam, so stop being silly. Go sit over there on the bleachers." And he pointed to where all of Mom's friends were sitting.

Then Dad went to stand with the rest of the fathers yelling hockey tips to their sons on the floor. The entire time Mom sat on the sidelines, hunched over, biting her fingernails. Every time my brother touched the puck she shut her eyes, hoping with all her might, that he'd scored. And if he didn't, she wasn't surprised. Mom thought *she* had made him mess up. And when the team lost, because they did, she felt that even more.

This was how Mom always felt when it came to winning things or doing well. She just expected the worst to happen because if the worst did happen, then she wouldn't be surprised or upset. Like before a test, Mom always told me not to expect to do well because then I wouldn't be so crushed if I didn't. It was a sad way to live, but to Mom it made sense.

"I knew they were going to lose," she said to me on the way to the car. Dad was busy giving Sam tips for the next game, and Mollie ran ahead to get a seat that would be far away from our sweaty brother. "I'm *always* right."

And it was true. Mom was always right—even when no one wanted her to be.

Dad's just a regular doctor for older people, so I didn't know much about surgery. What I did know I got from TV shows and movies. (Yes, the ones I watched while sleeping in my parent's bed when they didn't know I was up). Well, here's what I got:

1. Surgeons are very good looking
2. Surgeons talk a lot during an operation
3. Surgeons do anything they can to save their patients

I hoped Mom's doctor was just like the doctors in the TV shows and was good enough to fix Mom. Mom *needed* to be fixed.

I knew my family needed to go into the surgery with a positive attitude. Mom knew that, too. I guess that's why the night before she went to the hospital she called me into her room and said, "I know everything is going to be okay. I just need you to believe that everything is going to be okay." She pulled me into a hug and told me that I had to be positive—as if I hadn't heard that before.

I pulled away and looked at her face. For someone with breast cancer, she looked pretty good, and for someone who was going into surgery the next morning, she looked unbelievable. She did not have blue circles under her eyes, which was a sign that she'd been sleeping, and her nails were perfectly done and hadn't been bitten. Dad, on the other hand, was a mess. He was running around frantically packing bags, checking labels, and calling doctors making sure the next day's events were set.

The next morning Mom left for the hospital hours before I woke up for school. I felt her kiss me before she left, and I was pretty sure she whispered in my ear, "Be positive." She'd repeated this phrase millions of times over the past few days and adopted it as her motto.

The entire morning felt like I had been in a dream, and when it was time to go to school I willed myself out of bed checking the clock as I ran to the bathroom. It was 7:10 a.m. The surgery wouldn't begin for another two hours.

We began every morning in school with prayer. Normally, I used the time to give my notebook margins some extra decorations, but that morning I felt enveloped by the Hebrew words in our prayer books. I begged God to deliver my mom safely home to me and my siblings. I even paid extra attention during my Judaic studies, hoping to get some extra spiritual points. Still, I checked the clock every ten minutes hoping time would move faster. Every time I turned my head toward the flashing light on my wrist or my phone, I hoped some force of nature would make time move faster.

I couldn't even pay attention in class or when Hailey came over and asked me how I was doing. I had become a zombie, and the only thing I was capable of doing was dialing Dad's number on my cell phone. I called him every second I was free, and when he stopped answering, I called the rest of my family.

In the middle of class, my phone buzzed. I had told Mr. Dawn I would have to answer my phone in class, and he was okay with it. So I quickly ran out, nodding my head toward the teacher in a way that said, "I have to take this." Mr. Dawn nodded at me and continued his discussion on the importance of reading books and plays that were written almost a bazillion years ago.

Once I was in the hallway, I leaned against the lockers and picked up the phone. I took a deep breath as Dad said, "She's out."

"That's great news!" I squealed, trying not to disrupt the classes learning down the hall. But that was all I needed to hear to make me come back to life. "How did it go?"

"Everything went well. We'll be home in three days."

THREE DAYS! If I hadn't heard such good news a few seconds before, my head would have exploded. How could Mom not come home to me *now*? As soon as her eyes opened she should have been on her way back home. This wasn't fair. First, she got sick, and then she had surgery, and now she wasn't coming home.

I hung up with a loud snap and heard a crack. I didn't care if it broke considering it was the Emergency Phone. Zeidy, Mom's Dad, won it in a raffle a couple of years before and instead of choosing which kid to give it to, Mom said it was an extra phone in case of emergencies.

I walked back into my classroom, sat down at my desk, and pretended like it was a normal day again. I ignored Mr. Dawn's lesson. Instead, I drew a picture of myself and Mom reading a book on a beach a million miles away from everything going on here.

My picture came out lopsided and it looked like I was holding a serving tray instead of a book. I saw Hailey staring at it from over my shoulder. She saw I wasn't myself, but she didn't ask what was going on. None of my friends did. They left me alone. And that's how I was the rest of the day. I just stared into space thinking.

I thought about how much I missed Mom.

I thought about how much I wanted to see Mom.

I thought about how much it sucked to think positively.

And I thought about how much longer I would have to keep this up.

CHAPTER 14

I made a deal with Mom that I would stop bothering her with text messages and phone calls as long as I could stay home from school the next day. Well, I hadn't spoken to *her*. My grandparents thought I would aggravate her. Didn't they know speaking to me would probably magically heal Mom? It didn't matter though because I was staying home, and so were Mollie and Sam.

Even though I was taking the day off, I woke up early the next morning. The doorbell and phones would not stop ringing. I popped up in bed shouting. "Will someone please get the door?" I threw my blanket to the other side of me and rolled over. "I'm still sleeping."

And since no one got the door, *I* had to run downstairs in my teddy bear pajamas and open it. I usually always avoided the phone when it rang. Dad yelled at me for it, but I had to prove a point: if they weren't calling for me, I was not picking up. And who would call to speak with me so early on a school day?

"Hi. Flower delivery?" A tall man stood in my doorway holding the largest bouquet I had ever seen in my entire life. I had to show him where to set it because if I took it from him, I would drop it.

"Thank you so much. Have a great day." I said as I shut the door. Then I turned around to face the first floor of my house. Well, it didn't exactly look like my house anymore . . .

In the dining room, there were flowers *everywhere*. There were large bundles of red roses, blue tulips, daisies, and sunflowers. The flowers were in vases all along my dining room table. Some were so tall they were touching my ceiling. I felt like I was walking through an enchanted rainforest rather than the room where we usually ate dinner.

Then I opened the swinging door that led into my kitchen. The smell that hit me was very interesting. I looked at the table. It used to have black and white checkers with flowers on them, but now there were at least a dozen kugels on the table. I looked at the stove and noticed that Marta was already heating the chicken soup someone must have dropped off.

Whether you were friends or not, Jewish mothers *always* dropped off a kugel or chicken soup when someone was in need. It was nice to see how our community came together during hard times. Like after my Zeide died, we didn't eat anything but potato kugel for at least a month. The warm comfort food made the sadness feel a little less strong. I hoped it would help this time, too.

I walked deeper into my kitchen and found exactly what I was hoping to see. On the counter were completely untouched boxes of chocolates. But the box that stood out the most was wrapped in gold.

I spotted it. It was a beautiful box that had one written word on top of it: *Godiva*. My mouth watered just from looking at the beautiful label, and I just could *not* wait to open it and eat all the chocolates. But I would have to wait. There was one thing missing from the traditional get-well-soon gifts. So I walked out of the kitchen and into the living room.

Millions of helium-filled balloons floated in every corner of the room. It looked like one of those high school proms I always saw on TV had exploded in my living room. I sat down on the itchy plaid couch Mom never let us eat on and grabbed a red balloon by its string. I made a tiny hole with my fingernail and quickly put my mouth over it. The air was cold and tasted weird, but I wanted that wonderful squeaky voice to last over five seconds.

"Hello." I giggled in my new chipmunk voice. "I'm Alvin and these are the Chipettes . . ." The squeaky voice was gone. I put my mouth back over the little hole and sucked in more cold air.

If Mom were here she would have yelled at me saying, "Helium is toxic, Arianna! Do you know what that can do to your lungs?" But Mom wasn't here, and she wasn't going to be for two more days.

I looked around the room trying to figure out how many balloons I could cover over the next few days and how funny it would be if my voice permanently sounded like a chipmunk by the time Mom and Dad came home. I decided Mom *had* to hear how funny I sounded. I picked up the phone and dialed her number. Even if she didn't pick up, I could leave her a voicemail.

I sat wrestling with another balloon, trying to make the perfect-sized hole that wouldn't release so much helium before I could suck it in. Then I heard, "Hello?"

It was Mom!

"Mommy," I squeaked. The helium was still in my system. "I miss you. You have to see the house! It's a jungle in here! It smells pretty weird, but—" I was bouncing up and down on the couch, so excited to hear Mom's voice.

"Ari, I'm coming home." She interrupted me, sounding happy and weak at the same time.

Then someone took the phone away from her. "Hi, sweetie." It was Dad. "Let Mommy rest. She'll be home soon. If anyone calls don't tell them that she's coming home. It'll be our secret."

"Okay, okay." I understood. "Bye, Dad!" I threw the phone into the receiver. I was determined to make sure no one would bother Mom. I knew what I had to do.

"MOLLIEEE!"

I bopped away all the balloons that surrounded me and ran up to her room. It was still early in the morning, and Mollie was asleep, but I needed her more than ever.

"I need you, kiddo!" I slammed the door to her room open and hopped on top of her.

"I'm sleeping," she said as she tried to get out from underneath me. "Wake me in an hour." She looked so comfortable under her covers, but I shook that idea out of my head as I jiggled her awake.

"No, kid. I need you. Now!" I threw off her blanket and pulled her out of bed. I had a plan, and I needed her help before it was too late.

Together, we were going to soundproof our house.

CHAPTER 15

"I don't need to go to ballet tonight. Even if Mom makes me, I am *not* going." I glanced at Sam and Mollie who shared the same tired expression. We were sitting around the kitchen table picking at a bowl of blueberries for a snack.

Sam, Mollie, and I had spent the entire morning preparing for Mom to come home. It was much harder than we'd thought. Normally we made our beds, washed the dishes, and swept the floors before our parents came home. But not this time.

We spent hours unhooking every single phone line in the entire house. That took forever because the phones wouldn't stop ringing. Every time the phone rang, I picked it up saying, "Sorry, she isn't home, yet," and then I would slam it back down with a big smile because I thought it was going to help Mom. Mollie and Sam did the same thing, and by the time we were done, we were so tired, so sweaty, and so hungry.

"So, when do you think she'll be home?" Sam asked, popping a blueberry in his mouth. He seemed a little sad, but maybe he was just hungrier than I had anticipated and the blueberries weren't enough.

"Soon," I said. "Are you alright?"

"Yeah, I'm fine. A little hot and I wish we had some leftover pizza in the freezer." Mollie rested her cheek on the palm of her hand.

I glared at her. "Not you, Mollie. I'm talking to Sam."

"Oh." She slumped in her chair and put her head on the table, deciding this was not a conversation she wanted to be part of.

"Do you think it'll come back?" Sam asked.

"Do I think what will come back?"

"You know . . ." He looked around like he was telling a secret and then he whispered, "Cancer."

I hoped he didn't see how shocked I was the minute he mentioned *cancer.* "Wait, you know?"

"Well, yeah. Mom told me last week before I went to bed. She wanted me to know what was going on so that I wouldn't be so scared."

"Did you know, too?" I poked Mollie in the side.

"Now you're talking to me?" She picked her head up, interested. "Yeah. I know everything."

I laughed. She did spend a lot of time peeping through the cracks in the door and listening in on phone calls.

"And no one was going to tell me?" I threw my arms up and leaned back in my chair.

"I thought you knew."

Truth was, I did know. And I knew for longer than them, which made me feel closer to Mom. I also felt calmer knowing I wasn't carrying this secret anymore and everyone finally knew about her cancer.

"Do you think it'll come back, Ari?" He asked again. His voice sounded harsher this time.

"Cancer? No. Mom said that the doctors are taking *very* good care of her." He looked at his fingers and bit his lip. I could tell my answer wasn't enough. "And—and Mom promised that it was all going to be okay. She wouldn't promise that if it weren't true."

"You're right," Mollie chirped. Of course, I was.

I nodded at her, thankful for her encouragement.

"Yeah, I guess so," Sam agreed, but I didn't get the feeling he was so convinced that Mom was going to be okay.

Then the doorbell rang. Mollie, Sam, and I jumped. From the window, we saw it was one of Mom's friends. We thought we covered everything, but we hadn't considered a way to prevent the ringer. We were stuck. How were we supposed to tell someone who had driven over to leave?

"Are you kidding?" Sam moaned. He got up from his chair, but I motioned him to sit back down.

"When are people going to get it?" I turned to the door and yelled, "We don't want you to come—OUCH!" Sam hit my shoulder quickly, and very hard.

"She can hear you, Ari. Don't be stupid!" Then he swung closed the swinging door that gave us a clear view of the front door.

"It's also rude if I open the door and tell her to leave." I crossed my arms over my chest. Then I came up with a brilliant plan. "Let's hide, and maybe she'll just leave."

Sam rolled his eyes. "Whoever it is knows we're home." He popped a blueberry in his mouth and spoke while he chewed, "Where can we go? Mom's in the hospital."

"So then what do *you* think we should do?" I wasn't surprised my brother was acting like a know-it-all.

Ding-Dong. Ding-Dong. Ding-Dong.

This person really wanted to get into our house. But what if someone was just dropping off a kugel?

We decided our safest bet was sending Mollie to the door. Either way, she could play the cute little sister role or just play dumb. Mollie went to open the door while Sam and I peeked through the swinging door. We didn't want to miss this.

"Hi," Mollie said in her sweet voice as she opened the front door.

Standing in the doorway was Stacey—Mom's best friend in the entire world. If Mom cared about anyone more than her family, it was Stacey.

"Hi," Stacey said while attempting to walk in. "Your mom said she might come home early, and I wanted to check in."

But Mollie blocked her. She kept her hand on the door, making it extremely difficult for Stacey to even *see* inside. "No. She won't be home until Thursday," she said in her cute voice. She even held up two fingers to prove her point that she would have to wait two more days like everyone else. "So have a good day." She waved. "Bye!"

Mollie slammed the door in Stacey's face and turned around whisper yelling, "I think we're going to get into trouble for that."

I ran to her. "Cute kids don't get into trouble, Mollie. And you're way too cute!"

"That's why we wanted you to do this." Sam sat down on the stairs. "Ari always gets into trouble."

"Right," I agreed. And then realizing what he meant I added, "Wait, that's not nice." I swung my head around and gave him a mean stare. He ignored me and ran up to his room, taking two stairs at a time.

I turned to Mollie. "So, now that we're both home from school, want to make up a dance or something?"

Mollie looked at me and then at her feet. "I want to go to sleep," she said. "But I want to do what you want to do."

"Great!" I grabbed her and dragged her up to my room.

"What song should we use?" Mollie asked as she sat down on my unmade bed and crossed her legs into a pretzel.

"Do you even have to ask?" Taylor Swift's "I Knew You Were Trouble" blasted from my computer. We were both fierce followers of Taylor so we never had any issues deciding on what music to use for our dance routines.

I told her to stand up. She listened as usual and waited until I showed her the first counts of the dance I'd been thinking about before I went to sleep the night before.

She got the moves right away. Mollie was a natural dancer. She looked like Jennifer Lopez when she danced, just a little less inappropriate. Don't get me wrong, though. I was pretty good, too. My dance teacher even told me my feet were made for dancing. But most of all, I loved to make up dances and watch my vision come to life. So that's what Mollie and I always did. I told her what to do, and she *always* listened.

"One and two and three and four." I turned around to see Mollie dancing perfectly. I smiled and continued counting, "Five and six and seven and eight."

I paused the music and faced Mollie. "I can't believe I'm saying this . . . Mollie, you were so perfect!"

She didn't even try to hide how happy she was. She leaned against my closet door and smiled so big she glowed. "Thanks."

"I'm serious, Mollie."

I put the music back on from the beginning and watched Mollie dance by herself. Once she was done, I clapped and yelled "Woohooo!" making Mollie blush.

"It's no biggie, Ari. I've been learning from the best," she said before I started counting a new set of steps. But what she said turned my heart to mush, so I gave her a hug and a lunch break. I looked at the clock for the first time all day and realized Mom was going to be home soon.

When Mom came home I yelled, "Mom's home!"

I was so happy to see her and that everything was okay. I thought it was all over. She was healthy. Everything was going to be fine and normal.

"Ari, stop yelling." Dad sounded annoyed. "You need to be quiet."

"Right. I'm sorry. I forgot."

I really did forget I would have to start being quieter. It would be hard, but it was a sacrifice I would make for Mom.

Dad smiled at me and slowly helped Mom up the stairs. For a woman who had just been through surgery, Mom looked amazing. Her hair was a little messy, and she wasn't wearing any makeup, and her face looked a little too skinny, but her eyes were sparkling and she was smiling.

Once she was tucked into bed, my entire family went into the room and sat with her. We didn't need to talk to her; we just wanted to be around her. We watched her sleep for about an hour. Mollie sat on the floor by the bed and read a book while Sam, Dad, and I sat on the spinning chairs at the front of the room. We were all quiet for the first time I could remember, but then Mom's phone rang.

"Hello?" She picked up right away, her voice sounded groggy. "I'm just taking a nap right now. Can I call you later?" She hung up and put it on her night table.

"Mom, you just had surgery, and now you're going to start talking on the phone again?" I was angry, but I twirled my chair around so Mom couldn't see my face.

"Just let her rest, Ari," Dad said. "She needs a few days in bed before she'll feel normal again."

"But it seems like she's already back to normal." I pointed to Mom, who was reaching for her phone again. "She's texting!" I got up and stomped out of the room.

Mom was already talking to her friends after being home from the hospital for just one day. I loved her friends. I did. But didn't they understand I needed my mom? Didn't Mom know I needed her? I didn't want to share her with anyone. I guess that was the problem with having the most amazing mom in the entire world—everyone wanted a piece of her.

"Wait, Ari, I need your help with something." Dad ran after me. He stood in my doorway and watched me. I was opening my closet to get my pajamas out. Of course, I was slamming my cabinet doors closed just to show off how mad I was.

Instead of hugging me and rubbing my back the way he usually did to calm me down, he stood at my doorway and said, "Come help me change your mom's drains."

"Drains?" I had no idea what in the world he was talking about.

"Yes. It will be good practice for when you become a doctor." Dad had wanted me to become a doctor since the day I was born. But honestly, I wasn't sure what I wanted to do for the rest of my life. I couldn't tell Dad that, especially since he was a doctor. So I kept my doubts to myself. Mom told me I had to keep them a secret.

"Okay." I put my pajamas down and walked back into their room. I sat on the edge of my parent's bed. I didn't want to move around too much because I was afraid I would rip Mom's stitches open.

"What should I do?" I asked shyly, frustrated because I was useless.

"Just watch." So I did. I watched Dad reveal these little plastic tubes that came out of Mom's back. The stuff inside the tubes was red. I assumed it was blood.

"That is gross, Dad." I squirmed. I hated the sight, smell, and taste of blood. That would be a problem if I became a doctor when I grew up. I watched Dad empty the tube, connect it back to the chord, and place it back at Mom's side. "How does that feel?" he asked her.

"Much better." Her voice sounded weak, but her eyes were twinkling.

"Really?" I asked super excited. Maybe everything would get back to normal sooner than I expected.

"Yeah. I think I may try to walk around tomorrow." She sounded a bit weak, but she looked great. Then she turned to me and spoke as if nothing was wrong between us. "Did anyone stop by while I was gone?"

"Yeah, Stacey came," I answered and moved closer to Mom.

"What did she have to say?" Mom asked as Dad helped her sit up in bed. She winced a little, and Dad made an effort to move slower. He propped her up with some pillows.

"Is this okay?" He asked after adding a third pillow behind her head.

"Yes, that's enough, David." Dad kissed her on the forehead.

"She didn't say anything. Dad told us not to tell anyone that you were coming home, so we, um, kicked her out." Mom's eyes went wide with horror and I had to think of a way to reverse what I had said—and fast. "Well, Mollie did."

"You kids shouldn't have done that. I have to call her right away and explain." She reached for her phone again but couldn't touch it. Dad handed it to her, and she started texting as quickly as if the end of the world depended on her. "I can't believe this. And don't think you're getting out of calling her on your own to apologize."

"But I didn't do it!" I looked at Mom in shock. Of course, she was blaming this all on me when Sam and Mollie had just as much to do with it as I had. For some reason, I always took the blame. I think it was because I was the oldest girl in the house, so when she was gone I was in charge of what went on.

And of course, she was thinking about Stacey. Mom always thought of everyone else but herself. It was a very rare and amazing quality, don't get me wrong, but there were times when she just needed to think of herself, like two days after she got out of surgery.

I glanced at Dad who shared the same worried look as me. "Honey, can't you try and relax? You just got home." He tried to take the phone out of Mom's hands, but she shoved him away. Dad shot a what-can-you-do type of look and sat down in the twisty chair, taking out his own iPhone.

"Mom?"

She didn't even look at me. Instead, Mom said, "Please, Arianna, not now."

I left the room again just as mad as I had been before. I guess everything was getting back to normal.

CHAPTER 16

"Good morning, Mom. Thanks for waking me up," I said as I walked into my parent's room the next morning.

Mom had been home and cancer free for one whole night. I thought our daily routine would continue. Along with making me dinner and picking me up from school sometimes, I also thought that meant waking me up for school. What I found in my parent's bed, though, was not what I usually saw. Mom was fast asleep. Dad's side of the bed was empty, and I guessed it was because he was working while Mom slept.

I stopped in my tracks, frozen. Mom looked so vulnerable in bed. She was tucked between a million blankets and had a dozen pillows behind her head. She looked like the princess from *Princess and the Pea*. I mean, I knew she didn't have a pea underneath her mattress, but she must've had the same amount of blankets and pillows from the story. I could tell that right now she wasn't in any pain. And I was happy for her.

On any other morning, if I'd found Mom sleeping late on a school day, I would have jumped on her and begged her to wake up so she could make me breakfast and lunch and see me off to school. I also would have bothered her about forgetting to wake me up for the rest of the week. But this morning wasn't a normal case. Mom needed her rest, and I didn't need help getting ready for school. So instead of throwing a tantrum, I walked out of the room. I didn't even kiss her on her head.

I decided I would do something extra nice. I looked at my watch. I freaked out a little when I realized it was already 7:00. I only had thirty minutes to get my lazy brother out of bed and Mollie up and aware she had to be ready for school soon. I had a lot to do.

I tiptoed into Mollie's room. I felt a little bad about what I was about to do but it wasn't like she would get mad at *me* for waking her up. I threw her blanket off and Mollie moaned, twisted, and turned around her bed.

"What are you doing?" she yelled. Her hair was a mess, and there were saliva stains on the sides of her mouth. She slammed her body back down when she realized it was me. "Go away."

"You have to wake up." I looked at my watch. "It's 7:03."

"Exactly . . . I have time. Now go away!" She grabbed her blanket away from me and wrapped herself in it.

"Do you promise that you will be ready in time for school?"

"Do you think I can fall back asleep after the way you woke me up?" she whined. She made a good point. How'd she become so smart?

"You make a valid point. Goodnight, kiddo." I leaned down to kiss her on her head, just as she rewrapped herself beneath all her blankets and pillows. "Love you." I slammed her door as I left, realizing for a second that I had to be quieter if I didn't want to wake Mom.

Then it was Sam's turn. I had never experienced waking up a boy for school before, but I knew it was difficult from the sounds that came from his room every single morning. There was *a lot* of yelling, screaming, and a lot of door-slamming when Mom woke him up. Honestly, it was the noises that came from his room every morning that got me out of bed.

"Sam," I said as I opened the door to his room. I held my fingers up to my nose, defending myself from the smell that hit me in the face: sweat and feet. Then I saw his night table. It was filled with Laffy Taffy wrappers and empty bottles of Snapple.

"It's time to wake up." I tried to sound calm like Mom. He didn't answer me though. He didn't even move. He looked like a bear during hibernation, and if I didn't know any better I would've thought he was dead. Maybe he was in a sugar coma.

I decided to be more aggressive. I hit him on the back and shook him hard. "It's time to wake up." He didn't move. "Wake up!" He did and said nothing. "WAKE UP." I was frustrated, but I held back from pouring water on his head. I didn't want him to get mad and hit me back. That would hurt a lot, and a fight would probably wake up Mom. I decided to leave him and check on him on my way down to breakfast. So I turned the lights on in his room and said calmly, "Wake up." Then I went to my room to get dressed and pack my things.

When I was done getting ready, it was 7:18. Twelve minutes until the bus came. I checked on Mollie one more time and was pleased to see she was starting to get dressed. Then I went into Sam's room. He hadn't moved a muscle. I became angry.

"WWWWAAAKKKKEEE UUUUPPPPP!" I screamed so loud it was impossible for Mom to still be sleeping. I couldn't help it though, my hands were shaking, and though I couldn't see my face it must have turned bright purple. I didn't care. I told him so many times to just get out of bed, and he didn't listen. And the bus was almost here.

At that, he hopped out of bed and ran to the bathroom without even looking at me. He closed the door behind him as I said in a half-yell half-whisper, "You only have ten minutes."

I walked downstairs to breakfast, satisfied. I had done something good for Mom, and she had the rest of the morning to stay peacefully in bed. I had everything under control, and with a little more practice I'd have Sam out of bed so fast Mom would be impressed.

At 7:26 on the dot, I put my jacket on and tried to get Sam to come downstairs. "I'm leaving Sam. We have to walk to the bus stop, you know?"

"I'm coming, Ari, I'm coming." He ran down the steps, stomping on each one and making so much noise you would think an army tank was rolling around. He wore his backpack on one shoulder, his jacket was only on half his body, and don't even get me started on how messy his hair looked.

"You're going to wake Mommy up," I growled. "And we're going to be late." I opened the door to make sure the bus wasn't here yet. "And your hair?" I scrunched my face—the same face I made when I ate something I didn't like.

"Can you be quiet already?" He stared at me. But when he thought I wasn't looking he rustled his hands through his hair. I smiled. I knew he cared, even if it was just a little.

"Are you ready now?" I held the door open. He nodded as he followed me out. And right before I closed the door behind us, I heard a small voice shout from upstairs, "Have a good day at school, kids!"

It was Mom.

So much for giving her the morning off. I thought I was doing something nice by not waking her up, but of course, she was up. At least she didn't have to leave bed this morning. I was proud of myself for that.

When I got to school, Eva was being extra Eva-like on the other side of the classroom. She was sitting with the other poof-girls giggling about something and holding a piece of paper. I wondered what was on it that deserved such a laugh-out-loud moment.

I put my stuff down on my desk and then went to the back of the room where Hailey and Raquel were shuffling a deck of cards. I said quietly, "What's going on with Eva?" Before they could even answer, Zoe came over to us. "We heard that Mrs. Harbor is going to be late today so we're starting a game of Pig. Want in?"

"Sick." Hailey squealed. Then she pointed to me, "Ari wants to play. I'll watch."

I hated when she volunteered me for games. "I'm not in the mood today, guys."

"Fine. I'll play." Hailey rolled her eyes at me. I didn't know why but she suddenly seemed annoyed.

"What?" I asked her.

She waved her hands in front of her like she was throwing my question away and sat down in the circle my friends had formed. I sat next to her even though I wasn't playing.

"Raquel." And Zoe pointed to the cards as if they could speak for themselves. "You in?"

"Sure." Raquel shrugged and sat on the other side of Hailey. We started to play.

I became so interested in the game that for a second I forgot about Mom, Eva's annoying laugh, and Hailey's weird behavior. Then I heard a giggle so loud the boys on the other side of the school could have heard it.

I knew Raquel was just as annoyed as me because she snapped. She threw her cards on the ground and yelled, "What's so funny, Eva?" She crossed her arms over her chest and looked at Zoe with an I'm-sorry-for-ruining-the-game look. Zoe already understood what it was like to be tortured by Eva.

Eva perked up. Was she happy to finally get some attention? She turned her head to look at my friends and me playing cards. She smiled and walked over from her desk in the front of the room. She was still holding the mysterious piece of paper and waving it in front of her like a fan.

"I was on the bus this morning and someone gave me this piece of paper," Eva spoke to Zoe. "It must be annoying for you that Dylan told everyone that you like him." Then she handed her the piece of paper and sat on one of the desks closest to us. Her minions copied her, crossing their legs when Eva did. She continued, "I could tell him to stop . . . If you want."

"Oh. My. God!" Zoe's face changed from red to purple to blue as she realized what she was reading on the paper. "Where did this come from? I—I don't understand!"

"What is it, Zoe?" I got up and went behind her to see what she had read.

"Yeah. What happened?" Raquel looked over her shoulder to see what was going on. But Zoe had already crumpled the paper into a ball.

"It's the conversation. The one that I, um, had with Dylan, um, for the bet." Zoe was having trouble speaking. It didn't make any sense. The conversation that was written on the paper *never* happened.

"You never spoke to Dylan," I whispered to Zoe.

"I know," she whispered back.

I looked at Hailey who was the only person still sitting on the floor. She seemed just as confused as I was. None of this made sense.

"Wait. Let me see that." I took the paper from Zoe and flattened it out on my knee.

On it was a short conversation between my brother's screen name and Dylan's. And it wasn't even that embarrassing.

Here's how it went:

SG2247:	It's Zoe, how's it going?
DMW5768:	Hey...
SG2247:	I just wanted to let you know that I have a crush on you lol
DMW5768:	Lol! ☺

SG2247:   That's it?

DMW5768 has left the conversation.

Zoe had nothing to worry about because Dylan didn't even say if he liked her back or if he didn't. The real problem was the fact that everyone would see the conversation. And that Zoe never even started the conversation. I guess the biggest problem was that *someone* was lying.

"This makes no sense." Zoe put her hand on her forehead and looked at me. I understood that I should crumple the piece of paper before anyone else saw what it said. "I don't know who did this. I never said any of this!"

"But didn't you speak to him last week?" a poof-girl asked her, arms crossed.

"You told us that you did, Zoe," Raquel said. She was acting like the dumb bet was the most important thing in the world. They stood around Zoe waiting for her to answer.

Zoe looked at me for help and I nodded, motioning her to go ahead and tell them the truth. "I . . . I-I didn't okay? I couldn't do it. I was too nervous! But we weren't going to tell anyone." She was sweating. I couldn't help but think this all looked like a scene from one of my parent's grown-up TV shows.

"I told her she could do it," I chimed in and looked to Hailey, hoping she would say something that would help Zoe out. She didn't speak, though. She was looking at the floor. I knelt beside her when no one was looking and said, "I know who did it."

Hailey looked back at me like she was thinking the same thing. Then she pointed to Eva who was giggling on the desk like an evil witch. She thought she could control all of us and make us believe anything. I was sick of it.

I got up and spoke quietly, "Why would she make this up though? It's so mean." In fact, she had no reason to make Zoe look like a fool in front of the entire grade. And the worst part was that there was no way to even get Eva back. We could yell at her and tell her it wasn't nice to make up stories about people. We could explain to her that making up conversations between people that never actually happened in real life was not OK.

Suddenly, I realized I had done the same thing as Eva when I made Sam's status about her. I felt dizzy and I leaned on a desk chair to steady myself. I couldn't believe I had stooped as low as her. And there was nothing I could do to fix it without getting myself into trouble.

I needed to help Zoe get out of this situation peacefully. I went over to her as she paced the classroom. Raquel was trying to calm her down, but she wasn't doing a very good job.

"Guys, as long as we all know this is fake," I pointed to the paper, "then none of this matters." I spoke to Raquel and pleaded, "Can we call the bet off now?" I was desperate to get as much attention away from Mission Z as possible.

"I mean, we have no choice. Eva ruined all the fun." Raquel looked at Eva, got scared, and started re-shuffling the cards in her hand.

"Are you guys serious?" Eva stared at each of us as she got up from the desk. "Why are you guys always playing cards? You don't pay enough attention to what matters," she rolled her eyes and pointed to the crumpled paper. "I'm going to show this to everyone!"

Then Zoe got up. "I heard you like Mason."

"I was trying to avoid this," I mouthed to Hailey.

Eva froze and slowly turned around. "Who told you that?"

"Everyone knows."

"It was Sam's status on the portal the other night," Hailey finally spoke.

Eva looked like she was about to cry. "Guys, that's not funny." She stomped her foot.

"Well, it's not cool of you to make up conversations between people," Zoe said back.

"She's right," I mumbled under my breath.

"I—I'll stop. I promise." The poof-girls took a step away from her. They were probably afraid their leader was going to cry in front of everyone or that she would go far enough to throw a tantrum. The thought of either option was terrifying. "I *don't* like Mason."

"I don't like Dylan." I knew the truth, though. Zoe liked Dylan, and from the looks of it, Eva liked Mason. One hundred percent. No question about it.

"Why don't we just try to forget all of this?" I said getting between them.

"Ok, great." Raquel clapped. "Now that this is over with, can we please get back to Pig? Anyone ready yet?" Everyone sat down except for Eva and Zoe, who were staring at each other like they could read each other's minds. But I think both *were* thinking the same thing: this was over between them . . . for now.

Finally, Eva walked away with the poof-girls behind her, and Zoe sat back down to finish her game of Pig. My group ignored what had just happened and focused on our new game, which, for the record, was tournament-free.

I couldn't stop thinking about what I had started. In trying to help Zoe escape embarrassment, I had done the same thing to Eva that she'd just done to Zoe. I looked over at her. Eva was sitting with the poof-girls giggling. But her smile wasn't as bright and her poof wasn't as tall. Eva didn't seem as evil-like, and it was my fault. I rubbed my leg and played with my fingers, trying my hardest to look anywhere but at the card game at the center of the circle—after all, if it weren't for this deck of cards, none of this would've happened.

"Pig." Raquel yelped, startling my thoughts.

Even though I couldn't admit to Eva what I had done, I had to find a way to make it right.

Eventually, Mrs. Harbor walked into the classroom, breaking all the tension that was making the room feel extra hot, stuffy, and uncomfortable. And after sitting us down and getting us quiet, she stood at the front of the class and said, "The nurse wanted me to tell you girls that she is checking you for scoliosis tomorrow. Please wear a tank top, a bra, or anything underneath your shirt so she can check you properly."

At that point, a million hands shot up. We were all wondering the same questions: What was scoliosis? Why did we need to wear something underneath our shirts? And why would I *ever* take my shirt off in front of the school nurse? And instead of doing her job and answering our questions, Mrs. Harbor said, "Since scoliosis has nothing to do with what we're learning right now, I will not be answering any more questions about this. So please, girls, put your hands down." For once, we listened.

But she never said anything against passing notes in class. I opened my notebook, ripped a piece of paper out, and wrote, *What's scoliosis?*

I rolled the note into a little ball and threw it onto Hailey's desk, which was next to mine, when the teacher wasn't looking. I held my breath for a second as I watched the note fly in the air and in that same split second, I wished the note would land perfectly on her desk and the teacher would not see it. My wish came true.

Minutes later, I unrolled Hailey's reply that came flying at my head while my teacher was writing on the board. It said in red ink, *I think it's when your spine is crooked. I don't really know, but I think my sister has it, and her spine is crooked.*

I wrote back, *So why do we have to wear a bra?*

She answered me, *The nurse has to check your actual spine, and you can't be naked in front of the school nurse! That would be weird.*

I threw a note back at her that said, *Should I wear my sports bra?*

She answered, *I guess. I don't like this. I don't even wear my bra around my mom.*

Then I had enough of the crumpling of the notes and the secret passing and making sure my teacher didn't see me. I whispered to Hailey while my teacher left the room to photocopy some worksheets, "I'm so nervous about this. I don't know why."

"Arianna Goodman! Turn around and, for once, *please* stop talking!" My teacher yelled as she walked back into the classroom holding a bundle of freshly photocopied papers. I was caught.

CHAPTER 17

"Tell me if you need my help to balance," Dad said as he helped Mom out of bed.

It had been twenty-four hours since Mom came home from the hospital and exactly ninety-six hours since the doctors had cut her open. Now Mom was standing upright in her bedroom with a smile saying, "I'm standing."

My brother and I ran into the room right when we heard her. We had just gotten home from school and were still wearing our winter coats, but we didn't want to miss the excitement we'd heard upstairs. And what I saw in my parent's bedroom was *very* exciting. Mom was standing!

"Don't you think I should walk?" she asked Dad as she took two steps forward.

"Did the doctors do anything else besides fix your boo-boo, Mom?" Out of habit, I was careful not to say the word cancer in front of my brother. I sat down on one of the twisty chairs and shrugged my coat off.

It seemed like Mom had come out of surgery a completely different person. She was no longer afraid. Instead, she was walking to the bathroom. I guess I could say she was being positive.

"GO, MOM." Sam cheered as she walked slowly through the bathroom door. He ran to stand next to Dad who was smiling so big you'd think the Jets had just won the Super Bowl.

I was nervous, though. Was this normal? "Mom, maybe you should slow down?" I begged. I didn't want anything bad to happen to her. I couldn't have her go through more pain. I couldn't have her leave me again for another surgery.

"I feel great! I told you that everything was going to be okay." She was right. Everything was, so far, okay. Mom was home, walking. Now she was almost at the bathroom and hadn't tripped or fallen, yet.

"HELLOOO." A loud sound came from the door.

Sam looked first and said, "All right, I'm out." He escaped from the room.

I turned around, and I saw what he saw: a mob of people walking into the room. It was the kind you see coming out of a Beyoncé concert at Madison Square Gardens. Well, I'm over-exaggerating. It wasn't *that* big, but to me, it felt the same. It was irritating, and more than anything I wanted to get out.

First came Stacey. Then Ella, my mom's old friend from college who had an unusually big smile. Then Toby and Adalyn came in holding flowers in one hand and a box of chocolates in the other. And, of course, there were my grandparents who were frowning. They looked *really* unhappy. Probably because they thought the number of people surrounding Mom was going to aggravate her. Not going to lie, I was thinking the same thing, especially when they all started talking at the same time.

Stacey: "How are you feeling?"

Ella: "Does it hurt?"

Toby: "You're up and walking already?"

Adalyn: "I brought bagels!"

They rushed to Mom and huddled around her like they did at football games, only Mom didn't need another cheering squad—she already had one. Mom smiled at each of her friends, but I knew she was feeling tired and wanted to be alone. I wanted to kick them out so badly, but I couldn't. After all, I wasn't my sister. Bobby, on the other hand, was completely capable of doing just that.

Bobby was Mom's mom—a glamorous Eastern European lady who always had a blowout, pearls hanging around her neck, and heels on her feet. She had come to America from Hungary when she was in her twenties, met Zeidy here, and they built a family together. My grandparents would do anything for us, especially for Mom. That's why I trusted her to get Mom's friends out of the room for good.

"Girls, I think my daughter should have some rest. She just got home," Bobby said as she shoved Mom's girlfriends out the door. Mom told me that Bobby was known as the strict mom in high school so I knew she was tough, but I never thought she would be able to take on five concerned friends. At the same time, Dad helped Mom the rest of the way to the bathroom.

When she finally came out Bobby asked, "Honey, how are you feeling?"

"Good. I think it's time for my medication. Can you grab them for me? They're in the bathroom cabinet." Dad tucked Mom back into bed.

"Of course." Bobby went to get them, and Mom gulped them down.

"You should go to sleep, sweetie." She stroked Mom's cheek. It was weird watching Mom being treated as a child by Bobby. Especially, since I'd never pictured Bobby as an actual Mom. To me, she was the loving, caring, present-bearing Bobby. Continuing to act like Mom's Mom, Bobby turned to me and said, "And you should go out and let your mother rest." And she shoved me out the door like I was just another one of Mom's friends. "And take these bagels with you." Even the thickness of her Hungarian accent could not cover the disgust in her voice.

"Wait, I don't want to go. I want to stay with my mommy. I need to tell her about my day," I whined.

"Go tell your brother."

She closed the door in my face and locked it. I sat down in front of Mom's room and held my ear up to the door, listening for anything interesting. But I heard nothing. I crossed my arms over my chest and frowned. Once again, I was on the outside. I was determined to wait there until someone would finally let me in.

CHAPTER 18

"Next!" Nurse Virginia yelled from the bathroom inside her office, which was the size of a cardboard box. I couldn't even imagine sitting in there all day long because I would feel like I was stuck in an actual cardboard box. But Nurse Virginia sat in there every day giving kids Band-Aids, ice packs, and cough drops. She dealt with all the kids who complained about almost everything. And now I was just like them because after what I heard about the scoliosis examination, I was *not* going through with it.

Hailey was inside the bathroom with Virginia so I couldn't even wait with her, but Raquel and Zoe had already gone in. They said the examination was *so* weird. This is what Raquel said: "Virginia makes you take your shirt off and bend down and touch your hands to your toes—like I knew how to do that. And then Virginia puts her cold hands on your spine and makes sure that it's in a straight line. Then she makes you face her, so the entire front part of your body is showing. That's when she sees you in your bra. And you're completely topless in front of the school nurse. But apparently, she's required to do this to make sure your shoulders are straight and your back's not crooked."

Zoe said it was annoying because she wore a tank top instead of a bra and Virginia made her take her tank top off because she couldn't see her spine clearly through the fabric. Poor Zoe. She had a tough week.

Then Hailey came out. Virginia was waiting for me by the bathroom wearing a white lab coat that made her look extra professional. As Hailey walked out, she looked at me with really big eyes and said, "Good luck." I smiled at her and then walked toward Nurse Virginia.

Once she closed the bathroom door, Nurse Virginia faced me and said, "Take your shirt off, please." I laughed a little once it was off.

And then Virginia did everything Raquel and Zoe said she would. Her hands were cold, and her fingers tickled me the whole time they were on my spine, but for some reason my body felt numb. I couldn't feel my arms and legs. Maybe I was scared I would have scoliosis, but I think I would have known if my back was crooked or not. And I was pretty sure it was straight considering people usually complimented me on my perfect posture. But I was nervous about something. I just didn't know what. And then as Virginia made me turn around and face her, I figured it out.

But first, let me make it perfectly clear: being in a bra in front of the school nurse was not as bad as I thought it would be. I felt like I was wearing a bathing suit, except I wasn't covered in yucky-smelling suntan lotion, and I was nowhere near a swimming pool.

And second, I realized I was nervous that Virginia would find something wrong with me. Maybe I would end up like Mom. She had no idea she had breast cancer. The doctors had no idea she had breast cancer. But the entire time she *had* breast cancer. It was the same thing with scoliosis. Maybe I had it and no one knew.

The entire time Virginia examined me I held my breath, hoping I wouldn't have scoliosis. Hoping I wouldn't end up like Mom. Even after I put my shirt on, I held my breath. Well, I didn't actually stop breathing because then I would have either fainted or died. But I breathed more slowly. I held my breath until Virginia said, "You're good. Next!" And then she checked something off her clipboard and waited by the door for her next victim.

I opened the door to the little bathroom, stepped out, and finally took a deep breath. I felt so relieved that I was just another check off Nurse Virginia's list and nothing was wrong with me. I sat down in the waiting room chair to catch my breath when I realized Eva had been sitting there the entire time. She was next in line.

"What do you look so happy about, Ari?" She scowled. Her hair was not as poofy as usual and I wondered whether it was because she finally realized it looked dumb or because someone told her that it looked dumb.

"Nothing. Just happy that I don't have scoliosis." I smiled at her. She couldn't take away the fact that I was in my happy place, even if she tried her hardest.

"Oh." Thinking our conversation was over I got up from my chair, but then Eva said, "Was it scary?" She stared at her hands and shuffled her feet back and forth under the black waiting chair. Her pale skin looked extra pale under the fluorescent lights and compared to the white walls of the nurse's office.

Everything about her at that moment made her look vulnerable. I remembered how I felt when I had seen Mom tucked in so many blankets after surgery. She had been vulnerable then and it had been after a *real* surgery. Seeing that another person could feel the same way Mom had on a regular day of school made me realize that, surgery or not, people felt scared all the time. Maybe the reason people didn't walk around biting their nails or pulling their hair out of their heads out of fear was because they had their friends and family to hold their hands during the hard times. Like the way Mom had me. She had Sam, Mollie, Dad, and her parents, too. She also had her friends, though I didn't like to admit it.

But Eva was alone in Nurse Virginia's office, and I could tell she needed a friend. I shoved aside any bad feelings I had toward her and sat back down. Putting a hand on her shoulder I told her, "Honestly, it's not so bad. The worst part is when she sees your bra." Eva's eyes went wide and she flinched. I put my hand down from her shoulder. And for a moment I regretted being nice to her since she didn't seem to care at all. "What?"

"I totally forgot to bring a tank top!" She opened the top of her shirt and peeked inside. "I'm so stupid." She leaned her head against the wall and sighed.

"Zoe brought a tank top and the nurse made her take it off, anyway. She went right before me." Eva rolled her eyes, and I realized I wasn't helping. I wanted to leave so badly but couldn't abandon her. Nurse Virginia would yell "next" any minute, and Eva would not only be scared and alone but she would be braless.

Then a light bulb lit up in my head. "You can borrow mine."

"Gross." She scrunched her nose. "I don't want *your* germs all over me."

I pretended like I hadn't heard her. "I'll run to the girl's bathroom and change quickly. I'll be back in a second."

I ran to the bathroom and changed as fast as I could. I pulled off my nude sports bra and crunched it into a tight ball in my hand so that no one would see it as I walked back into the nurse's office. That would be even more embarrassing than being bare-chested in front of Nurse Virginia.

"Here." I held it out to her when I got back to the nurse's office. Eva tried her best to seem grossed out when she picked it up—holding it between two fingers and pinching her nose—but the hint of a smile on her lips proved that she was happy I was helping her through the mortifying experience of a scoliosis check-up. "This is gross. I should just put this in the garbage, you know, where it belongs," she said in a nasal voice.

I ignored her and focused on the fact that I could see she was smiling. "You're welcome, Eva. You can give it back to me whenever." And with that, I turned on my heels and left.

I felt good I had helped Eva out even if she didn't even seem thankful. I felt even better that I did not have scoliosis. And I was on top of the moon happy because I had finally made it up to Eva for Sam's status. Now, we were even.

CHAPTER 19

I'd never seen Dad cry.

Everyone always told me, "You are like your father with long hair." This made me extremely happy for several reasons. 1) I loved Dad. 2) I respected Dad. 3) Dad was the funniest and nicest man I had ever met on the entire planet. He was and always will be the Fun Parent. Whenever I needed a buddy to go with on a rollercoaster or watch a movie that was so scary I couldn't sleep in my bed for weeks, Dad came with me. This one time when Dad didn't feel well he still came with me on one of the sickest rollercoasters in the world: Kingda Ka in Six Flags, which is 456 feet high and reaches 128 miles per hour. No doctor in the world could argue that Kingda Ka was a step toward recovery, but Dad went on it with me anyway.

Basically, in all the years I'd known him—which was my entire life—I'd always seen him as the tough and strong guy that he was. It helped he was, in fact, a big guy. And I'm not saying *big* because he had a lot of muscle. Dad had a large stomach that resembled a globe. Yes, those round globes that spin in circles.

At first I didn't know if he was putting on an act. Honestly, I didn't know what to think. I was just surprised to see Dad cry.

When I got home from school that day, I still felt weird because of the scoliosis check-up. And Bobby and Dad had taken Mom to the doctor, so I had my parent's bathroom all to myself. I always liked having their bathroom to myself because Mom had so much makeup she could have opened a store.

So I went into my parent's bathroom and started putting on all her makeup just for fun. I always liked putting on makeup, especially while I studied; it helped me concentrate. It became a routine: the more makeup I put on, the more I studied. And when I was done, it became *very* clear how much I had studied.

Suddenly, as I was applying purple sparkles on my eyelids, the door burst open, and in came Dad. His eyes were red, and he looked seasick green. He headed straight for the shower, opened the glass door, and I heard a horrible noise. One of those belching sounds that you only hear when someone is about to throw up or when someone throws up. Turned out Dad threw up.

Once he finished, he picked up his head and realized he had an audience. And I was frozen in shock.

"Dad?" I put down the makeup and hugged him while he cleaned up. I turned the shower on to wash the remains of his past meal down the drain. From what I could see he'd probably had a very satisfying lunch. It was gross. "Are you okay?"

"Mommy needs chemotherapy," Dad mumbled as he turned the sink off. He choked as he spoke, and I thought he was going to cry again. He didn't though. Probably because I was standing there.

"What does that mean?" I realized that was a stupid question once I'd said it. Obviously, it was something bad, or else he wouldn't have freaked out.

"It means this isn't over, Ari. Mommy *still* has a boo-boo." He sighed and rested his hand on the gold sink knob and hung his head.

"You mean she still has cancer?" I asked and leaned against the cold bathroom counter.

Once I said the word cancer, I knew I'd said something wrong. He looked at me like I had said a bad word, but really I reminded him of the disease that was destroying his wife. I reminded myself of the disease that was *still* inside Mom.

Then the door to the bathroom opened, and Mom came in. She was wearing a white sweatshirt and red sweatpants. She looked cozy. She smiled once she saw me, and her eyes sparkled.

"Don't we get a say in this, Mom?" I crossed my arms over my chest.

Immediately, her smile faded. She stared at Dad like she already knew what had happened. He was hunched over the sink still looking like he was about to vomit. She ignored that. "What did you tell her, David?" Then she took a white towel from the cabinet and handed it to him. "We didn't decide on anything yet."

"But Dad told me that you need chemotherapy, whatever that is. And that the cancer isn't gone and that means you—you lied, Mom!" I was hysterical.

"Wait," Dad left the bathroom as she started to explain. "Just because I'm getting chemo doesn't mean that I'm not okay. We want to make sure that the cancer is gone for good. Everything's going to be fine." She tried to hug me, but I pushed her away. I realized I shoved her too hard when I saw her wince. I almost forgot that she had surgery only a week ago.

"I'm sick of you telling me that everything's going to be fine, Mom. It isn't." I grabbed the door handle and threw the door open.

"Didn't I tell you that you had to be positive, Ari? It *is* going to work out." She tried to calm me down, but I wouldn't listen. And she tried to chase after me, but she was too weak.

"No. It's too hard!" I yelled as I ran through her room.

"I promise everything will be okay. You just need to have faith that it will be."

"But how can you say that, Mom? You have cancer." And I slammed the door shut before she could answer me and ran straight into Sam. His eyes were wide, and that's when I realized that I yelled too loud.

"She still has it?" Sam asked slowly. "Does she still have cancer?"

Sam's face turned so pale he looked like a ghost. He looked like his worst nightmare was coming true.

"Ari! Sam! Mollie! It's time to light the menorah. Come down!" It was Bobby. I could see her short brown hair from the top of the staircase. Just as I had originally suspected, we had completely forgotten about Hanukkah. I bet there were no latkes or presents. This was no time for a celebration.

I ignored Bobby and nodded to Sam. "It's true."

Just then, Mollie walked out of her room. *Great*, I thought, *now she's going to find out, too*. I decided I'd handled enough stress for one day and explaining chemotherapy was Mom's job. Maybe one day she would explain it to me too. But I knew one thing for sure: Mom was still sick.

Sam's eyes turned watery and I didn't want to be there while he cried. Just like I'd never seen Dad cry before today, I'd never seen Sam cry either and I didn't want to. And even though Mollie seemed too little to even understand what cancer was, her face seemed so sad. She looked crushed.

"Go talk to Mom," I said to them.

I stomped down the steps, ignoring the judgmental stares Bobby gave me.

CHAPTER 20

Hanukkah is the holiday that commemorates the time that the Jews revolted against their Greek oppressors. In school, we focus more on the miracles—the fact that a day's supply of oil kept the menorah in the temple lit for eight days straight. If that is not a miracle, then I don't know what is. Anyways, I had always learned that spreading the miracle of Hanukkah was the point of this holiday, so we lit the menorah on our windowsill in our living room. This way all the people driving and walking by were able to see all four of our menorahs lit for the first night of Hanukkah.

I took a candle in my hand at the same time as Dad, Sam, and Mollie and placed it on the right of the Menorah. Then we each took another candle that was designated for lighting the other candles.

"Dad, I'm scared I'm going to burn myself," Mollie whispered.

"Don't worry, sweetie," He kissed her on the top of her head. "Sam, watch your sister as she lights."

Sam switched places with me so that he could watch over Mollies candle-lighting skills. I always wondered how this holiday was never considered a fire hazard.

Bobby and Zeidy stood behind us with their arms wrapped around each other.

"Ready kids?" Dad looked at each of us.

"Why are we doing this without Mom?" I asked.

"Please, Ari, just light the candles. I have a surprise for all of you afterward," Bobby was always trying to shut down my arguments.

"You mean you have presents!" Mollie was sold. "I'm ready, Dad."

Dad lit all of the candles we were holding. And then we started to sing. We chanted the blessings as we lit the first candle and placed our candle in its position at the center of the menorah, with four spots on each side. I looked in awe at our flames dancing together in the window. In just seven more nights all eight candles on the menorah would be lit. That was always my favorite night. There was so much light and excitement.

By the time we got to the last blessing, we were dancing around in a circle and singing. My grandparents got involved too, and before we knew it, we were circle dancing (known as the hora).I was smiling and laughing so much that I almost forgot why Mom was upstairs and was not able to celebrate with us.

"Alright kids, time for the next surprise," Bobby sat down on the couch and motioned to Zeidy to do the same. We sat on the floor around them, crossing our legs and looking up at them. *What was next?*

"We know that this year is a little different for you kids, and we wanted to make sure that you still felt the spirit of Hanukkah. Your Zeidy and I don't normally believe in giving presents on this holiday, but we made an exception for this year."

And with that Zeidy pulled out three beautifully wrapped gifts from under the couch.

"Wow!" Mollie exclaimed as she jumped toward the biggest one. Of course, *she* got a present that was larger than her entire body. She ripped the wrapping paper with all her might, making crazy "oohs" and "aahs" as she went. I hoped for her sake the large box lived up to its expectations. I could tell Bobby was holding back every bone in her body from helping Mollie open the present like a proper lady.

"Mollie, would you like some help?" She tried to stop the madness, but Mollie just shook her head and continued.

Sam took one look at his present and ran to the kitchen. I guessed that Bobby had made him some ultra-oily potato latkes and given him an extra $20 to justify his gift.

"Ari," Zeidy looked at me. "What's wrong?"

I suddenly realized that I had not even touched my present. It was sitting in front of me with beautiful blue wrapping paper and a golden bow perched at the top. I stared at it as if my glares would make the gift open on its own.

"Nothing," I shrugged. I took the box in my arms and played with the gold ribbon.

"Ari, sweetie," Zeidy knelt beside me. He tucked a piece of hair behind my ear. "Mommy is strong. You don't need to be afraid."

I looked at Zeidy and the wrinkles that lined his face. I called them wisdom lines, only to myself. I learned the hard way that you can't bring wrinkles up to an old person. But I believed that the older you were, the more wrinkles you had, and the wiser you must be. My Zeidy was *very* wise.

"I *am* afraid, Zeidy," I sighed. I looked at Mollie and Bobby playing with her gift. Mollie had been dying for a pink fluffy blanket to put on the edge of her bed. Now she finally had one. I was excited to snuggle with her and her new present later that night.

"Look at me, sweetheart." So I did. "There are so many things in life that you are going to worry about. There are some things that you can control and some things that you can't, and it will be hard. But one thing you can always rely on is how *you* feel," he pointed to me and then continued. "When things are hard, it is easy to be sad. What makes you, my darling, special is that *you* can also choose to do something about your situation and change how you feel."

I was confused. I thought this conversation was going to go in a different direction and Zeidy was going to yell at me for being selfish and sad. Instead, he was complimenting me.

"Your mother told me how you woke up Sam and Mollie the other day for school so that she could sleep a little later. She told me how you tried to shoo away her friends to make sure she got home to a quiet house. Thank you, Arianna, for taking care of my daughter when I can't always be there for her." He paused for a moment, "But don't be disrespectful to her friends. They love her as much as you do."

"You-you think *I* am taking care of Mom?"

"Yes. By smiling and being by her side, you are helping her heal. Don't you understand? It is not just about the medicine right now. We have to be there for your Mom in all senses. We have to help my daughter get better," Zeidy sighed. "I would give anything for one more day with my mother. I know how this must feel for you, Arianna, but you are doing everything you can. I am so proud of you. Now open your present, we have latkes to eat." Zeidy's eyes sparkled and his wisdom lines deepened. I jumped into his arms and gave him a huge hug. Suddenly, I felt Mollie and Bobby's arms around us too.

"Is anyone going to join me for some latkes?" Sam yelled from the kitchen. His mouth sounded full.

"I'm going to get some latkes before Sam finishes all of them," Mollie said as she pulled away from our hug.

"I'll put some more up on the pan just in case your mother wants to eat one before she goes to sleep."

"Thanks, Zeidy," I said.

"For what? You haven't even opened my gift yet."

He was right. So I ripped off the blue paper and revealed what was inside. It was the GHD Platinum Styler. The hair straightener that I had been eyeing for months.

"THANK YOU!" I jumped on him. "Thank you, Bobby," I yelled toward the kitchen. I finally had some heat to tame my hair. I couldn't wait to try it out the next morning. "I'm going to show Mom." Without thinking, I ran upstairs, stomping on every step to the top.

"Mom! Look what I got," I stormed into the room.

"Shhhh!" Dad whisper yelled. I hadn't even realized he had left us after we lit the candles. "She's sleeping."

"Oh right," I shut the door and slumped my shoulders.

"Ari," it was Zeidy on the top of the stairs waiting for me, "Let's go eat some latkes. It'll make you feel better."

Without saying a word, I took his hand and followed him to the kitchen where Sam, Mollie, and Bobby sat. And just as he had predicted, they did make me feel better.

CHEMOTHERAPY

CHAPTER 21

I began my mission to discover what chemotherapy was and why it was such a big deal. I needed to find out why Dad got teary-eyed every time Mom brought it up and why I almost started World War III with Mom because of it.

First stop: Dad. I thought since he was a doctor, he would know what it was. I asked him to explain it to me, but he spoke in his doctor's tone and said so many medical terms in one sentence that I just got confused. And because I was completely lost, and his words gave me a headache, I walked away.

I went to Mom after that and asked her what chemotherapy meant, but we ended up getting into a fight after she told me it would make her lose her hair. How could she not think *that* was a big deal?

Then, because no one in my family was able to explain it to me in a way my brain could understand, I turned to the only thing in the world that could answer anything, at any time, in any language, and in any place . . . well, with Wi-Fi. My best friend Google told me chemotherapy was "the treatment of a disease by the use of chemical substances." That didn't sound bad, so I kept reading.

There are these little sponge balls that grow into much bigger animals like giraffes or lions when they are kept in a cup of water overnight. And that's basically what cancer is—when a lot of cells in the human body grow quickly. And the only way to stop them from growing is to kill the cells. Basically, doctors try to kill the floating giraffe sponge that grows in the glass in the bathroom.

Anyways, chemotherapy—also called chemo—kills all cells that grow fast in the body, like hair, nails, and, of course, The Evil Beast Cancer Disease. Chemo also makes people feel sick. And I'm not talking about the type of sick people fake when they want to get out of school. It's the don't touch me, don't move me type of sick when they're vomiting their brains out, and they get so skinny people think they look like a skeleton. So from what I read on the Internet, that was what I understood. And from my experience, I could say no one should believe *everything* they read on the Internet.

Now, back to Mom. Before starting her chemotherapy treatment, Mom had to take a lot of tests. I'm talking about blood tests. These tests gave results that decided on the future—sometimes to say whether someone was sick or not and other times to decide what to do when someone was sick. This time, the second one was Mom's case.

After deciding to do chemotherapy, Mom had to take a test to decide what kind of chemo she would take. Normally, I wasn't nervous before she took a test, and usually, she didn't even bother telling me when she was going to get one because they happened so often.

She said, "I'm warning you when you get home from school today you cannot come near me. The doctors are putting chemicals in me that could be bad for you if you come near me." She saw my confused face and realized I didn't understand why she was telling me this. "It's for your safety, Ari." Something about this test was different.

"What do you mean, Mom? What are they putting in you?" I wanted to ask her a million other questions, but I was going to be late for the bus. She never warned me before she was getting a test. Tests had become routine in our house. They were as normal as my weekly spelling tests. Something was different this time and, of course, Mom wasn't telling me the full truth. Once again, I was on the outside.

All she said was, "Nothing that'll hurt me. I promise, Arianna, I'm going to be okay. Just if you come too close it may hurt *your* chance of having children one day."

Then I heard Sam and Mollie fighting for the bathroom, and we only had five minutes to make it to the bus stop. I hugged Mom and ran to make sure Sam wasn't late for school. I left the house confused and angry.

There was no way I wasn't going to touch her later, and that thought got me through the day.

Finally, I was home from school. After the day I'd had, I was so excited to just *be* home. Mr. Dawn made me frustrated when he asked us to draw a picture of the one person in the world who made us the happiest. And I wanted to draw Mom, but then he told us we couldn't draw a family member. My entire class just stared at him after that. We were all thinking the same thing: who else in the world could make us super happy? Obviously, some girls started to draw Taylor Swift or Zayn Malik, but I had never been so interested in pop stars.

I ended up drawing a picture of Marta. She was almost part of the family, but Mr. Dawn didn't know that, and she did a lot of the same things Mom did. And she always gave me food, and that made me happy.

Either way, the class frustrated me, and I was really excited to be home. Except when I finally got home and found a party of people. The whole gang was there—Dad, all four of my grandparents, and Mimi. And to my surprise, they were sitting in Mom's room . . . with Mom. I *thought* no one was allowed to go near her.

It was like the Marshmallow Experiment. Almost fifty years ago, a psychologist named Walter Mischel decided he wanted to test how children would respond to instant gratification. So he put a marshmallow in front of them and waited to see if they would take it right away or wait for the doctor to give them the marshmallow. The child was told to wait to eat the marshmallow, and if he did wait, he would be rewarded with an *extra* marshmallow. There was a catch, obviously. The child had to wait with the marshmallow sitting in front of him. The marshmallow would just be sitting there, in front of the kid, taunting him, "Eat me. Don't wait." Based on the results of this experiment, Mischel predicted that if the child waited the appropriate amount of time for the marshmallow, he would get better SAT scores when he was older. And if the child took the marshmallow right away—because what kid is going to wait?—apparently that child would have lower SAT scores. That was the experiment, in a nutshell.

Well, Mom was my marshmallow. She was sitting in the room right in front of me and I wasn't allowed to go in. The more I thought about not going near her, the more I *wanted* to go near her and the more the idea that other people could go near her bothered me. By then, so much frustration was bottled up, that I was a shaken Diet Coke bottle destined to explode.

"Hi, Mom." I was standing outside her room with my arms crossed over my chest. I was channeling my inner tween being overly dramatic and sensitive, once again. "Why is everyone here?"

"Hi, Ari," Mimi said. She was sitting in *my* twisty chair. "How was school?"

I put my hands on my hips and narrowed my eyes. "Why are *you* here?"

Dad walked over to me and put his hands on my shoulders. "They already have kids. We just don't want you to have problems in the future. Go downstairs and eat dinner with Mollie and Sam."

"Mollie and Sam aren't home." Sam was at his friend's house, where he spent most of his time these days, and Mollie was at a tennis lesson. "You should know that." I bit my lip, trying to fight back tears. I wanted to be with Mom. I was jealous the rest of my family could be with her.

I whispered to Dad, "Will she be like this forever?"

He smiled, which I took as a good sign. "Of course not. She just has to . . . pee out all the chemicals that are in her." He thought I was going to laugh at how silly that sounded, but I wasn't in the mood.

"What are you talking about, Dad? I just want to see Mom."

I threw my hands in the air and bounced up and down on my heels. I was extra annoyed. Why did everyone always treat me like a baby? I was affected by Mom's cancer as much as everyone else in the room. I deserved a chance to be there too. But everyone made it clear they were not letting me in, so what could I do?

I gave Mom one more pleading look but when she didn't say anything I stomped to my room and slammed the door, which according to Walter Mischel counted as not taking the marshmallow. I guess my SAT scores would be stupendous.

I threw off all the pillows on my bed—three large striped ones, two polka-dotted ones, and a little one with a bow—then threw my body onto my bed and hugged myself until I was warm. I cried hysterically, and the only thing that was going to make me feel better was Mom.

"I want Mommy." I sobbed. I hoped Mom would feel so bad she would come out of her room and hug me until I stopped. Nothing happened, though. Dad didn't even come in to see if I was okay.

After what felt like an eternity of waiting for someone to check on me, I was still crying, but I was also tired. My eyes were puffy, and my face was sopping wet, so I was excited when I heard the door to my room open. Hoping to see Mom, I picked my head up. It was Bubby—Dad's mom. She came to see how I was doing.

"Ari," she opened the door. "Why are you crying?"

I didn't answer her. I wanted her to leave, especially if she didn't understand why I was crying. Normally, Bubby always knew what to say to make me feel better. She usually took me for ice cream. The man working at Häagen-Dazs eventually recognized us and knew our orders by heart. I always got chocolate chip on a cone and Bubby just got chocolate in a cup. If only she had ice cream on her at that moment, maybe I would've calmed down.

"Arianna." She walked over to my bed, sat down, and rubbed my back. "Mommy can't come here right now, but she told me to tell you that she loves you."

Again, I didn't answer her. I just wanted her to leave, and if she wasn't going to, then I was. "I want Mommy to come here . . . NOW!" I screamed as I ran out of my room, across the hall, and into Sam's room. I threw myself on top of his bed and cried even louder.

At that point, everyone in Mom's room came into Sam's room to see the show. They stood at the doorway with arms crossed and disappointed looks. They seemed mad, but I kept crying.

"How can you aggravate Mommy like this?" Bobby said and then turned to walk out of the room.

"How old are you, Arianna? Act like a big girl!" Mimi told me.

"Mommy's tired so be quiet," Gramps yelled at me.

"I'll give you money if you stop crying." Dad was the only one trying to be nice. He sat on the bed next to me to show me he cared. Still, I was sad and hurt, and my entire family was yelling at me. I *needed* to explode. I got up from the bed and yelled even louder. I jumped up and down and threw my body onto the floor. I was burning with adrenaline that numbed the pain coming from my sore throat and throbbing shoulder.

"Just bring her to me . . . PLEASE." I banged my hands on Sam's brown leather couch, and all the decorative pillows fell on the floor around me.

My family looked at me in disgust. I knew what they were thinking: how could I behave this way while Mom was sick? Still, they just stood there like statues. And then something changed in their faces. Was it pity? Or sympathy? I realized it too late. It was fear. I was yelling too loud to hear her, but during my tantrum, Mom came out of her "hiding place" and into Sam's room. Her eyes were burning with anger and because I wasn't used to that look, I crawled back on my knees to be farther away from her.

"ARE YOU HAPPY NOW?" She came close to me so I could see every wrinkle on her face and the spit flying from her mouth as she yelled, "I'M OUT OF MY ROOM. ARE YOU HAPPY?"

I was too afraid to cry. I sat down on the couch and hugged my knees to my chest. "I'm . . . I'm sorry. I . . . I didn't know . . . what else to do." I managed to say between sobs and stared at the pillows on the floor. I just didn't want to look at her.

"Well, I hope this was worth it!" She looked at me with shame and embarrassment.

I looked at the rest of my family in the room hoping someone would chime in to help me. When Dad saw my face, he mouthed so only I could see, "I told you to stop."

"Say sorry to your grandparents." She pointed to my family. "And if you ever . . . EVER act this way again, I'll punish you so badly." Her face softened for a second while she spoke, "I know that you're sad, but I'm not okay with the way you are acting."

Then she stormed out of the room just as loudly as she had come in. My family gave me one final look-what-you-did-to-Mommy look, and then followed her out too.

I was alone.

Before I went to sleep, I opened Mom's door and said, "I'm really sorry for the way I acted. I hope you can forgive me." Apologizing was the right thing to do. I had to start taking responsibility for my actions. And especially in this case, I *was* wrong.

The room was dark so I couldn't see her face, but Mom's voice sounded hurt. "I need to see a change in your behavior. You can't keep throwing tantrums the way you did tonight."

"I really am sorry. But do you still love me?"

"I always love you even when I hate the way you're acting," Mom said as Dad let out a loud snore. I couldn't help but giggle.

"Goodnight, Mom."

"Goodnight." I closed her door.

Even though we made up, Mom and I didn't talk before I went to school the next morning. I thought we could use some space. As I sat on the bus to school, I had a feeling that something bad was bound to happen that day.

"Eva's looking for you," Hailey whispered as I walked to my desk.

My eyes widened and I gulped. Why would she be looking for *me*? "What do you think she wants?" I spoke quietly as I put down my books and sat. Suddenly, the room was spinning, and I didn't feel so well.

"I don't know, Ari. But from the look on her face when she told me to find you," she shuddered, "I can tell that it's not going to be good."

"What kind of look was it?"

"I think it's better not to show you," Hailey said dramatically and rubbed my back.

"Seriously, Hailey, I do *not* need this right now. I got into a *huge* fight with my mom last night and I—"

"Arianna, I need to speak to you ASAP." It was like she came out of a magic pink bubble. Eva was suddenly looming over us with her hands on her hips and her hair poof reaching the sky.

"So I heard."

"Hailey, do you mind giving us a minute?" Eva glared at her.

She nodded. Before leaving, Hailey gave me a look of sympathy. She squeezed my shoulder as if to say, "good luck."

"Let's get this straight." Eva sat down at Hailey's desk and leaned in so close I could smell her coffee breath. When was it too young to start drinking coffee? "SG2247."

I froze.

"Ring any bells?"

"Yes," I whispered, hoping she wouldn't hear me.

She knew. SG2247 was Sam's screen name. The same screen name that had the status revealing Eva liked Mason. I lowered my head so she couldn't see the guilty look on my face. Because that's what I was: guilty.

"At first, I was surprised Sam made his status about me. I mean, if I liked Mason, I would've just told him myself, obviously," she said, feigning confidence. "Then I realized you and your friends were logged in to Sam's account the night the status appeared. Why did it say that I liked Mason on his status? *I* wasn't part of the dumb bet. No one was supposed to know *I* liked anyone."

She suddenly stopped speaking. I guessed she wanted me to give her some explanation. I didn't want to lie anymore. But I didn't want to tell her the truth. I was panicking. I looked into her eyes, hoping she would give me a sense of what I should do, but what I found was the same vulnerable expression I'd seen in Nurse Virginia's office.

And I realized I had to tell her the truth.

"I did it." Eva flinched. Was she shocked I admitted it? Or was she relieved it wasn't Sam and his friend playing a prank on her? "I was wrong and I shouldn't have done it. I'm sorry."

"You can't just say sorry and make this all go away, Arianna. I mean, Mason knows I like him now. He knows."

"Well, do you like him?" I asked her even though I knew the answer. She probably did.

"I don't!" She lied.

"Then who cares what Mason thinks," I said and leaned back in my chair. Finally, I felt free from my secrets. A weight had been lifted from my shoulders.

"Who cares?" Eva's voice was harsh. This conversation was not going according to her plan.

"Exactly."

"Sorry to interrupt but Mr. Dawn is here," Hailey said pointing to our teacher at the front of the class. "I sort of need my seat back."

Eva's face turned scarlet red as she popped up from Hailey's desk yelling, "This is just great! Mason knows I like him and it's *your* fault and all you say is sorry? And I have *your* dirty bra in my bag."

The room around us went quiet. Everyone heard her outburst. Everyone knew she liked Mason now. At least this time it was not my fault. Eva had no one to blame but herself.

"Eva," Mr. Dawn sounded calm and stern at the same time. He was not one of those teachers that threw students out of the classroom for interrupting, but he also did not have any patience for girl drama. "Do you need a moment outside?"

I didn't know someone's skin color could turn such a dark shade of red and I didn't know Eva could ever become speechless. She just stood by my desk like a statue. To my surprise, I felt bad for her.

"It's my fault," I heard myself say. "I made a bet with Eva that she couldn't get the entire class quiet even if she tried." I stood up next to Eva. Why was I helping her? "I guess I lose, Eva. Look at that... Everyone's quiet!" I forced myself to give her a pat on the back. "You win."

Eva gave me a nervous smile and linked her arm through mine as if we were best friends. "We're sorry, Mr. Dawn. We didn't mean to distract the class." She smiled and flipped her hair to seem innocent and sweet. But I saw through the act.

Mr. Dawn raked his hands through his hair and leaned against his desk. At least he seemed happy Eva's meltdown was a fake out and he didn't have to deal with our pre-teen drama. He was silent for a moment while Eva and I just stood there. "Just please sit down so we can start class." He pointed to our seats. "Girls, please don't disrupt me again." With that, he clapped his hands and began his lecture.

"What was that about?" Hailey whispered while Mr. Dawn wrote on the board.

I timed my response carefully so Mr. Dawn wouldn't catch me breaking class rules twice in one day. I turned to her and lied, "Nothing."

Hailey raised her eyebrow but didn't ask any more questions about what had happened between Eva and me. When I looked down there was a pink piece of paper lying on my notebook. I opened it under my desk, careful that Hailey wouldn't see.

I guess I owe you for this one. Thanks.

There was no signature and I didn't feel the need to respond. I folded up the paper and quickly put it under my notebook.

I looked at Eva sitting two seats down from me. She was smiling. "I really do have your bra in my bag," she whispered a little too loud.

Mr. Dawn turned around. "Girls! Please stop talking!"

We were caught and, this time, there'd probably be an extra homework assignment as a result. But I didn't care. I was too happy. I was finally behaving in a way that would make Mom proud.

CHAPTER 22

The next week, I was passing by Mom's bathroom when I heard a buzz. At first, I assumed it was Dad shaving his scruff, but then I remembered seeing him eating dinner downstairs in the kitchen. I walked toward the bathroom and leaned against the cold mirror that covered the door. I heard people talking:

"It was smart of you to cut your hair now," a voice said.

"I guess so. I hope it's not too noticeable," a second voice replied nervously. I froze. The second voice was Mom.

I assumed Mom was cutting her hair before it completely fell out from the chemo. It wasn't all completely bad, though. Chemo was going to kill the rest of the cancer that was inside Mom.

She had a choice between a chemo that would be longer, less aggressive, and allow her to keep her hair, or a chemo that would be shorter, more aggressive, and make her hair fall out. As a family, we decided on the more aggressive one. She would get four treatments of chemo over the span of two months. That meant that every two weeks, Mom would go to the doctor and have needles attached to her for a very long time so the chemo could get inside her. She would feel sick while the chemo did its thing, but Mom was a trooper and could handle it. We had never thought so positively.

But this was all happening so fast.

I barged into the bathroom. I was shocked when I saw all of Mom's dark hair on the white marble floor. What *was* left were short spikes that stood straight up. She sat on a black chair while Joanne, the hairdresser, stood behind her holding scissors.

"Why didn't you tell me about all of this, Mom?" I pointed to the hair on the floor.

"I'm just cutting it before it all falls out," she said to the mirror.

"Yes," Joanne said as she put her scissors down and smiled. "We thought of a few things that we could do once it grows back." I made a face, but Joanne didn't get the hint to stop talking. She rustled Mom's hair, and I could tell she was becoming scissor happy. She continued, "I'm thinking highlights."

I ignored her and spoke directly to Mom. "I guess I'm the only one in the house who's going to have curly hair now."

Mom used to have beautiful black curly hair. In college when large hair was in style, she told me she had the puffiest and curliest hair of all her friends. Her hair was so large it extended beyond any picture. And even though styles have changed, Mom's hair looks beautiful blown straight, which is how she wore it.

I always felt that I was the lucky daughter to inherit Mom's thick curls, and although I didn't always like to wear it curly, I was proud to have curly hair because Mom had it too. She always found gel for me and packed my hairbrush when I went away. We always tried new shampoos or conditioners, hoping some product could help our hair seem less frizzy for even just a moment longer. And even though none of the products we bought ever worked, I felt better wearing my hair curly with someone else.

This time Mom looked at my face like she understood why I was upset. "Joanne said that I'm going to need some amazing products to keep control of my hair now that it's short." She spoke calmly while Joanne cleaned up. "I'll need your help with that, Ari."

"But do you think that your hair is ever going to grow back to normal?" I wasn't interested in making Mom's hair look better. I was only concerned with her old hair and when it was going to grow back.

"I think eventually it will. Still, you might just get used to my hair looking like this," she touched the spikes at the top of her head and I frowned.

"You think so?"

Mom's face suddenly lit up and her mouth curved into a huge smile. Hopping up from the chair and grabbing my hands, Mom exclaimed, "Come on! We could have fun with this, Ari. Come with me tomorrow. I'm going to the wig store."

"I have school tomorrow, Mom." I was a little annoyed she didn't already know that.

"You can miss one day. The school will understand. And I really would love to have you there." Once again, the roles were reversed. Mom was acting like the child and, for some reason, I was acting like the responsible one.

"Fine. If you *really* need me, I'll miss a day of school for you." I had always begged Mom to let me stay home from school before she had breast cancer. This time she was begging *me* to miss a day of school. How could I say no?

The next day Mom took me to *The Human Wig Shop*, a store at the center of town that sold the nicest wigs—that's what Mom told me. We walked inside, and a bell rang telling the owner we were there. I walked around the store.

There were rows and rows of all different types of wigs: long and short, curly and straight, blond and brown. All of them were placed on top of white foam heads that had eyes, a nose, and a mouth. It seemed like all the "heads" were staring at me, and it made me nervous. I wondered if Mom was going to buy a wig that looked like her old hair or go all out. This was an opportunity for her to change her look. Then again, it already had changed—her hair was only three inches long.

Then a skinny woman with orange hair came out from the back. Mom went up to the counter. "Hi, I spoke to you on the phone earlier. I'm beginning chemotherapy this week, and I need a wig."

"Hi, I'm Heather." She stretched her hand across the counter. "What kind of wig are you looking for? I think we can match your hair color, but some women like to get a few different styles."

Then Mom and Heather got into a whole discussion about hair lengths and colors, completely ignoring that I even existed. This stuff didn't interest me, though, considering I was still mourning the loss of Mom's curls. So I walked around the store admiring all the wigs. I touched a wig and then touched my hair to see if I could feel a difference. I couldn't. I knew the hair wasn't real. Mom knew the hair wasn't real. And Heather knew the hair wasn't real. So how come I didn't *feel* a difference between the hair on top of my head and the wigs on the foam heads?

"Ari, tell me how this looks." Mom must have suddenly remembered I was missing a day of school for this and motioned me over to the counter where she stood holding two different wigs. I listened, and we ended up spending two hours trying on different styles, eventually settling on three different ones: a long dark brown curly one, a long dark brown straight one, and a short dark brown one. The last one was my favorite because when she tried it on she put on a pink barrette, and it made her look like she was a model from Paris. Mom also bought a pink barrette and a few scarves to wrap around her head for when the wigs became too uncomfortable.

Although we left the store satisfied with our purchases, I couldn't help feeling guilty. I had hoped that if Mom wore a wig, things would seem more normal. But nothing, not even fake hair, could do that.

CHAPTER 23

Even though I hated answering the phone, when I got home from wig shopping, I tried something new and picked it up the minute it rang.

"Hello?" I said into the phone in the living room. I was in the middle of making up a dance with Mollie, and it was the closest phone to me.

"Hi!" I laughed, realizing it was Hailey. The one time I picked up there was a person who actually wanted to speak to me. The universe was always playing tricks. "What's up? How was school today?" I didn't miss not being in school. I mean, I missed my friends, but it was good to spend a day with Mom. Plus, I wasn't really in the mood to sit in class trying to make it seem like I was listening to my teachers.

"Are you going to sit on the phone now?" Mollie puffed out her bottom lip and folded her arms across her chest.

I put the phone on my shoulder the way Mom always did while she was multi-tasking and said, "Give me five minutes, Mollie." I leaned back on the couch and ignored the fact that Mollie had stomped away. Then I realized Mom was napping and said, "Don't stomp, Mollie, you'll wake up Mom." I put the phone back to my ear. "Sorry about that. Mollie was being annoying."

"No worries." Then she switched gears. "School was so fun. Guess what we watched today? Guess, Ari?"

Hailey seemed super excited, and I thought I knew why. They had shown the *Period Movie*, and I missed it. I didn't know whether to be happy I missed that hour of torture or sad I missed laughing about periods with my friends. Everyone always acted like the *Period Movie* was so bad, but deep down it was sort of an accepted right of passage into the sixth grade.

"You watched the *Period Movie* today, didn't you?" I slumped deeper into the couch. "I didn't know that we were going to watch it today. I would have come to school!" I whined, feeling bad that Hailey had to listen to me. I twirled the phone chord around my pinkie and watched my finger turn purple.

"No. Don't be upset," she sounded less enthusiastic. "It was gross actually, and Mr. Dawn was the one to introduce the movie to us! Can you imagine that? The entire cast from the musical *Annie* put on a little show for us, telling us what a period is, how to use a tampon thingy, and how to keep our bodies clean. It was funny . . ." She paused and then continued, "But you didn't miss anything."

I could tell Hailey was trying to make me feel like I hadn't missed out. I had, though. Watching the *Period Movie* was disgusting, but it was something I had wanted to watch with my friends. And I had missed it and it was because I was with Mom. Because *she* had cancer. The next time I'd be watching a period was when I got *my* period. I shuddered. It was too gross to even think about.

But I couldn't help but think this was another thing in my life that was ruined because of The Evil Breast Cancer Disease. If Mom didn't have breast cancer, I wouldn't have skipped school to help her buy wigs, and I would never have missed the movie.

"I'm not upset, Hailey. I just . . ." I watched my finger change colors as I continued to twist the chord.

"What?" Hailey asked.

And then I untangled the chord from my finger. "I'm sick of this. I miss my mom being my mom. I miss her waking me up for school and sitting with me at the dinner table when I get home from school. I just want things to be the way they used to be, and right now it just doesn't seem like it's going to get any better."

I felt like I was going to explode. Not because I was angry this time but because I was sad. I was just sad, and I couldn't think anything could make me feel better except saying why I was sad, so I did.

"I just wish that my mom never had breast cancer in the first place and my life would go back to normal. I would be able to hug my mom so tight she'd pop, my dad wouldn't always look like he was about to cry, and Sam and Mollie wouldn't fight me to get Mom's attention. I just don't see any of that happening ever again."

Then Mollie came back in saying, "Are you talking about me?"

I put the receiver on my shoulder so Hailey couldn't hear me. "Ugh! No, get out!" And I threw a pillow at her.

She dodged the pillow and said, "Come hang out with me."

I put the phone back to my ear and sighed.

"Arianna . . ." I didn't expect Hailey to say anything that could make me feel better. And I could tell she didn't know what to say. She didn't know what it was like to be in my shoes. "I'm here for you. And your mom is doing amazing. Everything is going to be okay, Ari. You missed that dumb movie, and that's it, and your family isn't going anywhere. In a couple of months, everything will be back to normal, hopefully. I know they will so you have to know that, too."

I took a deep breath. "You think things can go back to normal after this? Hailey, my mom had . . . no, she still *has* breast cancer."

"I mean, I'm no doctor so I have no idea what's going on inside your mom right now, but I think the point is that you have to sort of make yourself believe that it's going to be okay." And when I didn't answer she continued. "My grandma died of cancer last year, and I never thought that my mom would be okay after that. She loved her mom so much. I never saw her so sad. But if you look at my mom today, would you ever notice something like that happened to her?" She paused for a second and then answered her question. "No, Ari, you wouldn't. You have to stop feeling so sad or else you'll forget how to be happy."

"Yeah, but my mom is getting chemo tomorrow." I should have stopped talking at that point. She must have felt uncomfortable hearing me complain about how Mom was sick and how my life was changing. After all, everyone had something going on in their life, as Hailey said. I wasn't the only one with a problem. But I couldn't help myself and I continued to feel sad and talk to Hailey about it.

I was so afraid of what chemo would do to Mom, and the only person I could talk to was Hailey. She was the only person in the world I could say the word *chemo* to who wouldn't burst into tears. Yes, I had mentioned *chemo* to Sam that morning and he had burst into tears. He was sensitive.

"And she's still going to be okay, Ari. Chemo is going to help her. I heard my mom talking about it with her friends when my grandma was sick. She said that it makes you sick for a while because it's so strong that it kills all cancer inside of you. It's a good thing, Ari." Hailey sounded like she knew what she was talking about. She also sounded a little bit annoyed. I bet she was fed up with all this cancer talk.

"You know what?" I thought out loud and jumped up from the couch.

"What?"

"I think maybe you're right."

"You know I'm right. Okay . . . enough. Listen to this." And just like that Hailey took my mind off everything. She said, "Eva has gotten much better ever since the Zoe-Dylan Incident. Do you think she's embarrassed she made such a big deal about it and no one cares?" I hadn't even realized Eva hadn't told us a story about a boy since I had lent her my sports bra in Nurse Virginia's office.

"Actually, I heard something crazy. That Eva was in the boys' hallway and—"

"Of course she was." I sat back down on the couch.

"Yeah, so she was there, and *Mason* went over to her and told her that all the boys were wondering why she was always hanging out on their side of the school."

"WHAT?" My body tensed. Suddenly, I felt bad for Eva. "Who said that? And what did Eva do afterward? I think I would have run home and cried in bed. That's just too embarrassing." Even though I felt bad for her, secretly I was happy someone told her to stop running to the other side of the school.

"I don't know the details. I overheard the boys sitting behind me on the bus talking about what happened. I don't think Eva would want us to hear *that* story, so she won't be telling it to us anytime soon."

"That's so sad . . . but I bet Mason has a crush on Eva and that's why he's being mean to her."

"Wait, now you're rooting for her? What happened with you two? You never would've felt bad for her if this happened before you became best friends in class the other day."

"Eva and I are *not* best friends. Come on, Hailey, you know that."

"Just don't link arms with her again. It creeps me out," Hailey giggled, and I was happy she believed me.

"And I do feel bad about what happened. I mean, that's beyond embarrassing!"

Then Mollie came in shaking her head. "You're the worst," she told me.

"Don't be silly, Mollie." I patted the seat next to me. "Come here." Then I said to Hailey, "Listen, I got to go. See you tomorrow, and thanks for everything."

"Sweet dreams," she said and hung up the phone.

I turned to Mollie. "So what do you want to do?"

She finally sat down on the couch. Her mood quickly changed from angry to happy in a matter of seconds.

"Whatever *you* want."

I rolled my eyes. "Of course."

"Actually," Mollie bounced up and down on the couch, "what's a period?"

I didn't let her see me hesitate—I wasn't used to her disagreeing with me—and there was absolutely no reason for an eight-year-old to know what a period was. "What? Who told you about that?"

"You did." She pointed to me and bounced up again. "I *always* listen to you and Hailey talking on the phone."

"Are you kidding?" I wanted to kill her. But then I looked at her cute face and realized it wouldn't hurt either of us if I told her what it was. As long as she kept it a secret, of course.

I sat back and talked to Mollie like she was a fifth grader. I told her about Mission Z and how I thought Zoe actually liked Dylan and that's why I didn't make her message him the other night. And we talked about how weird it was to like a boy and what it was going to be like when I got my period. Her eyes got wide whenever I said period, but she never giggled. I was impressed.

After like an hour, which was a long time to talk seriously with someone I always viewed as a little kid and who I normally used as a guinea pig for my dance routines, we decided it was time to go to sleep.

"Promise you're not going to tell anyone what I told you, Mollie?" I asked her before going to our separate rooms. "All of it. Including the boy drama," I narrowed my eyes and lowered my voice to a whisper, "It'll be our secret." I held out my pinky and waited for her to hook her pinky around mine to solidify our pinky promise. But Mollie stared at my pinky with a blank face.

"Why's your pinky in my face?" She raised an eyebrow.

I laughed. "Haven't you ever done a pinky promise?" I took her pinky and wrapped it around mine to demonstrate. "There. Now it's permanent."

"My first pinky promise," she said staring at our connected pinkies. Mollie's face brightened, and she clapped her hands. She whispered, "Secrets are fun."

I laughed. I guess secrets could be fun. Sometimes.

"Good night, Mollie."

"Good night, Ari."

As I got ready for bed, I realized how awesome Mollie was. She helped me completely forget about everything with Mom and that the next day was Mom's first day of chemotherapy.

CHAPTER 24

For everyone else, Tuesday meant another normal day at school. But for me, once again, Tuesday was not normal. It was the day Mom would get her first chemo treatment.

Mom woke me up that morning to give me a hug and a kiss. She told me she would be home later feeling lightheaded and nauseous and that I shouldn't be afraid. Of course, I tried to fight with her to let me stay home from school. She said it would be a good distraction for me to be with my friends, so I stopped fighting. She pulled my blanket up to my chin and stroked my hair. She blew me one more kiss as she tiptoed out of my room and shut the door.

In school, I wasn't surprised that Mom was right. School *was* distracting. And it wasn't until 1:00 in the afternoon—the exact time of her appointment—that I became nervous.

At that exact minute, I turned my head away from my teacher and looked out the window. I watched the seagulls fly over the blue ocean and then at the surfers riding the waves. I wanted to be one of those carefree surfers, and then all I would wish for was sun and waves. That seemed simple compared to the number of things I was wishing for. I couldn't help but think how much my life had changed and how at that exact moment it would change even more. Mom already warned me about the effects of chemo, and I had a feeling it would be far worse than what she was telling me. Nobody wanted chemo, and there was a reason.

Hailey broke my train of thought. She was standing over my desk. "Do you want to come over next week to watch *The Voice?*"

I jumped and looked around. No one was there. "Where's everyone?"

"It's recess, Ari. But do you?"

"Right . . . right." I blinked twice and shook my head to get my thoughts back on track. "I was just spacing out. But, yes. Have you watched lately?"

"Of course! Blake Stone is *so* cute." Hailey squealed, jumping up and down.

The Voice was something my family always watched together. We would cozy up in my parent's bed and laugh at the singing contestants who sounded terrible and tried out just to be on TV. But we hadn't had much time to sit together to watch reality TV lately.

"Me too. And Christina is also just so pretty. My mom said that—"

And then everyone came back into the classroom, and Mrs. Harbor clapped her hands yelling, "Recess is over, girls. Settle down."

We sat and listened to Mrs. Harbor describe our upcoming assignment. "Girls, I'm feeling a little bit generous, and I've decided to make this assignment more *fun*." She leaned forward and widened her eyes as she spoke. She raised her hands, faced her palms outward, and wiggled her fingers—a movement I liked to call jazz hands—to bring more spirit to the class. She seemed like she was already having more fun, and if *fun* was contagious, we'd be jazzing our fingers all around the classroom in a matter of seconds.

Mrs. Harbor stood up and walked in between the rows of desks, wriggling her fingers as she talked. "I want each of you to choose a character from Tanakh—you can choose anyone, even if we have not learned about his or her story yet. Then, you're each going to find a partner and create a poster that highlights the similarities and differences between the characters that you've each chosen. Don't forget that I give points for creativity, girls.

"And also because I'm feeling generous this assignment is due at the end of March, which gives you about a month to complete your work. Since you have more time, I have higher expectations." She made hand motions that looked like she was raising a bar to show us that she was, in fact, raising the bar.

At that point, a million hands shot into the air. Each girl had a question of whether they *had* to create a poster and if not, could they make a mobile or a diorama? Everyone wanted to know if they could triple-up and many girls whined that they would rather complete the assignment on their own instead.

This gave me a perfect opportunity to whisper to Hailey, "Hey, want to be my partner?"

"Didn't think you'd have to ask," Hailey whispered back. Of course, she was going to be my partner. She always was. Lucky for me, Hailey was a very talented artist.

"We can do it in two weeks so we have plenty of time. I can bring a poster, and I know you have a lot of markers at your house," I said to Hailey. Mrs. Harbor was still distracted by my class's mini-freak attack.

"Sounds like a plan."

And then Mrs. Harbor decided she'd had enough excitement and began lecturing about the origin of the Hebrew language. I wished she stuck with the jazz hands.

Later, when I got home from school, I ran to Mom's room and wasn't surprised to see her fast asleep. Wrapped in layers of white blankets, the only part I could see was spikes of black hair. I wondered how long it would take her hair to completely grow back. Or, I guess, for the rest of her hair to completely fall out. Next to her, on her night table, were bottles and bottles of pills. Each bottle had a different label and was supposed to be taken at a specific time.

I heard a toilet flush, and then the bathroom door opened. Out came Stacey. "Hi, sweetie. How are you doing?" She gave me a big hug, thinking that was exactly what I needed to make me feel better. "If you ever need anything," she put her hand on my shoulder, looked at me seriously, and told me, "call me."

That's what everyone always said to me. They knew I would never actually call. It was the natural role of the friend to offer the girl with the sick mom any help that she needed. I wished they realized the only thing I needed was for Mom to get better. That wasn't something I could get from a phone call.

"Thanks so much, Stacey." And just to show how grateful I was, I said, "I will." I smiled. Then she sat down in *my* twisty chair, leaned back, and relaxed.

"How was school, Ari?" Dad walked in and went straight to the side of Mom's bed. He gave her a quick kiss on the top of her head and stepped away.

"It was fine. Mrs. Harbor gave us a project today and—"

"Before I forget, I was in charge of her afternoon pill. I gave it to her like two hours ago. I hope that's okay," Stacey said to Dad.

"Yeah, that's okay. Maybe we should leave the room and let her rest," Dad said, and we listened. We all headed toward the door just as Bobby walked in.

She quickly hugged me and gave me a sloppy kiss on my cheek that I immediately wiped off. Like Dad, she went straight to the side of Mom's bed to see how she was doing. Mom wasn't awake, but Bobby went ahead and gave her a wet kiss on the top of her head anyways. Dad cringed.

She turned to him and said, "I gave her the afternoon pill a couple of hours ago while you weren't around. Then I left to pick up some food for dinner. It's down—What?" Bobby looked confused as she looked from me to Dad to Stacey. The three of us were standing still and silent. My mouth dropped to the floor. Stacey and Dad exchanged glances.

Stacey broke the silence when she clutched her stomach and cried, "Oh my god! I killed her."

"What?" Bobby said with an extra hint of a European accent, so the "w" sounded more like a "v" sound. "What's going on? Someone tell me." Her face paled and her eyes became watery.

"I gave her a pill almost two hours ago, too." Stacey paced the room. "We gave her the same pill and I . . ." She trailed off and continued to pace.

"Oh my god. What does that mean?" Bobby stared at Stacey with dagger eyes, who—for the record—seemed completely checked out and was no longer listening to Bobby. Bobby shook her hands above her head and sat down putting her head between her knees. She looked up and spoke to Dad. "David, get your head out of the clouds and tell us what we should do."

"Dad, what are we going to do?" I asked. I was worried, but I didn't fully understand the concept of pills, so I wasn't freaking out. I stood on the sidelines and watched the scene play out: Bobby yelling at Dad, Stacey walking back and forth, and Mom sleeping in bed. It's crazy to believe that Mom depended so much on the people around her when she was sick, because when she was healthy she hated accepting other people's help. The tables had turned. But if something happened to Mom because of it, I don't think she'd be too happy. I mean, if anything happened to Mom, after all those surgeries and chemotherapy, I wouldn't know what to do.

"It's funny that everyone thinks I know the answers because I'm a doctor," Dad said to me in a half-whisper. By the looks of it, Dad didn't seem too concerned.

I laughed nervously at Dad's joke. I guess as a doctor, things like that happen all the time. Still, she *was* his wife. It especially didn't help when all he said was, "It's fine. We'll wait until she wakes up. Everyone relax, and please leave my wife alone. Don't try to give her pills, please. Leave that to me."

He shoved us all out of the room and made some calls on his cell phone. There was the concerned Dad I knew. But Bobby and Stacey wouldn't leave without a fight. They continuously apologized to Dad while also bickering with each other.

"Oh no," Dad yelled from the bedroom, and all of us ran back through the bedroom door.

"What happened now?" Bobby seemed afraid to ask. She shut her eyes.

Dad poked his head out of the room and said, "You guys woke her up. Please just leave."

But before Dad shut the door I saw out of the corner of my eye a little woman lying in bed. She was covered in puke.

CHAPTER 25

Right before Mom's first surgery, I slept at Bobby and Zeidy's house a lot—mostly because they lived only five minutes away from my school, and because I was scared to look at Mom. A few days before the surgery, my grandmother stopped her car right in front of the school and refused to let me out. She claimed I looked really sad and I had to tell her why. She started by saying, "When your mommy was a little girl, I had a hip replacement. It's an extremely major surgery. I think I told you that story before." I nodded. Bobby *always* told my siblings and me stories about her past. "Before the surgery, Mimi came into my room at night and told me that she was afraid I was going to die." She paused and looked at me seriously. "Are you afraid that your mom is going to die?"

I wasn't expecting a question like that. Didn't anyone realize I was still only in fifth grade? And it was also before eight in the morning. But I told her the truth. "I told Mommy that I was afraid she was going to die a million times. I'm afraid." And then my grandmother hugged me and sat with me until I had to go to school. For some reason, she was the first person to make me feel like there was some hope that Mom was going to be okay.

That's what I thought about as I watched Bobby cry in the kitchen. She kept sobbing, "I killed my daughter! I killed my daughter!" And even worse, Stacey still didn't leave.

I felt like it was my responsibility to hug Bobby and make her feel that everything was going to be okay just like she had for me. It was weird for me to try to make someone like Bobby feel better about something I was also sad about, but I had to help her. I didn't completely realize Mom mattered to more people than just my family—like the people who lived with me. And it was okay for Bobby to be sad about Mom because Mom was her daughter. She meant the same thing to Bobby that I meant to her. And if that was true, then Bobby loved Mom a lot.

So I rubbed her back while her head rested on my shoulder and repeated over and over, "Everything is going to be okay. Just like you said it would be." After repeating that after what felt like a hundred times, I felt like Mom before she went into surgery. And I even started to believe everything *was* going to be okay. I guess I wasn't just convincing Bobby. I was convincing myself.

I was right. Mom was okay, and neither Bobby nor Stacey had killed her. Still, to prevent future accidents, Dad told me to put a sign on the door to their bedroom that explained the following rules:

1. No one can wake up Mom if she is sleeping
2. No one can give Mom pills even if it is the specific time of day for her to take pills
3. No one can sit on Mom's bed whether she is sleeping or awake

That last rule became an issue the day after The Pill Incident when Sandra decided to snuggle up next to Mom and fell asleep. None of us knew at the time, but Sandra was coming down with a case of the flu. What if she had passed that horrible disease to my already sick mom? Some people would just do anything to be close to Mom, and I was no exception.

CHAPTER 26

I finally got to spend time with Mom a few days after her first chemo treatment. It was the first day the phones weren't ringing, Dad wasn't constantly sitting with her, and her friends weren't bugging her to get some attention. It was finally just Mom and me.

"Hi, Mommy," I said as I sat down quietly on the chair across from her bed. She looked pretty good despite the fact she was pale as a ghost.

"Hi, sweetie. Can you pass me a tissue, please?" She sounded so weak, but I resisted the urge to run toward her and hold her until she fell asleep. Instead, I got her a tissue from the bathroom and handed it to her. I watched as she blew her nose slowly, and for the first time, I saw how skinny she was. Her face was the smallest I had ever seen. "How has school been? How are Hailey and all your friends?"

I couldn't remember the last time she had asked me about school or silly things like friends. "They've been really good. I'm going to Hailey's house next week to do a project that Mrs. Harbor. . ." Sam and Mollie burst into the room. Being interrupted was becoming a habit.

They said hi to Mom and sat down on the chairs next to me. Then Dad came in with a huge smile and kissed Mom on her head. He sat down on the edge of her bed and checked his watch to make sure it wasn't time for her evening pill.

"Hey, Mom," Mollie said. Sam looked sad, and I hoped he wouldn't ruin Mom's mood by telling her whatever he had on his mind.

"How was school today, kids?" Mom asked with a smile as she sat up in bed.

Dad continued to stare at Mom on the edge of the bed. He seemed happy just staring at her. "This is nice, isn't it?" he said in his cute voice. "All of us are finally together. I think this is the first time since the surgery that no one is around."

"I tasted the mushroom spinach kugel downstairs. The one that looks weird, and everyone is afraid to touch. It wasn't so bad," Sam spoke up.

"I can't believe you tried that." Mollie nudged Sam and her face wrinkled in disgust. "You're gross."

"I think we have to write thank you notes to everyone who gave us food." Mom ignored the bickering while she spoke.

Dad rolled his eyes and looked up from his phone. "We do not have to *write* thank you notes. Why can't we just call everyone to say thank you?"

"Well, if you don't," Mom squinted her eyes and cocked her head to the side while she threatened, "I'm not going to go to my next treatment." With that said, she got up, walked to the bathroom, and shut the door.

"She always does that," I said, annoyed, and got up from my chair. "Why does she always have to do that?"

"Doesn't matter anyways, Ari. She *is* getting that treatment," Dad said. And then he turned to Sam, "Three more to go, baby!" And Sam slapped him high five. Great, now we were a cheering squad for chemotherapy.

"All right, I have to go do homework," Sam said as he left the room. I followed him out. Before I left, I turned toward the bathroom and called, "Love you, Mom."

Once I was out of the room, I followed Sam downstairs to the kitchen. "Hey?" I asked. "What's wrong with you?"

"Nothing. Leave me alone, please." He was picking at the chicken that no one put away after dinner.

"No." I sat down next to him to prove my point. I wasn't leaving.

"Leave me alone," he said as he turned the other away.

"You know I'm not going to leave you alone until you tell me what's wrong, so just tell me."

He sighed, "Fine." He looked like he was going to cry. "You have to promise not to tell anyone. *Especially* Mom."

"I promise." I leaned in closer.

"I had a math test at the beginning of the week, and I studied a lot. I was nervous because that was the day Mommy was getting her first treatment and I . . . I didn't do so well."

"Well, what did you get?" Usually not so well meant in the low nineties or high eighties, so I was especially surprised when he looked at the floor and said, "I got . . . I got a sixty-five."

"OH MY GOD." I honestly could not believe my ears. That was almost a failing mark.

"Well, you don't have to make me feel worse." He pushed his plate of chicken away. "I don't know what to do and don't want to bother Mom and Dad about it either."

I felt weird trying to make my brother feel better because usually he was the one who always made me feel better. "First of all, you have to stop moping around. You're supposed to be the tough guy. Second, we are not going to tell Mom or Dad about this. They don't need to worry about our grades right now. It's not a big deal, and it is a one-time thing and . . . Wait, it *is* a one-time thing, right?"

He nodded.

"So next time you're going to study—"

"But I did study." He seemed frustrated.

"So next time you're going to study harder. Got that?" He rolled his eyes. I didn't think he appreciated the pep talk, so I gave him the next best thing. A hug. We hugged for a while until I felt he was okay and until he didn't want to hug me anymore.

He looked at me and said, "I've been trying to pretend that Mom's not sick to make it easier for me. When I realized I couldn't tell her about my grade because it's not fair to make her worry about silly things." Sam hesitated and looked at his fingers while he spoke, "I don't know, I guess I realized that I can't pretend anymore. Mom is sick."

He looked up from his fingers and breathed deeply. He seemed relieved after admitting the truth. I couldn't imagine how hard it must've been for Sam to keep in all his feelings all the time. He was the opposite of me—the minute I felt something, anything, I let everyone around me know it too.

"But Sam, it's a little late for that. Mom's getting better."

We sat in the kitchen for a while, listening to the ticking of the clock and the buzz of the light bulbs, in silence. Sam didn't touch his plate of chicken again and for once in my life, I had nothing to say.

"Mom's getting better." Sam broke the silence.

"I told you that already. I can't believe people think you're smarter than me."

"Don't start with that now. I'm trying to be serious here for a second."

"Alright, Sam." I moved to the chair that was across from him and leaned forward on the table. "I'm all ears," I said cupping my ear to prove my point.

"No. It's just that I didn't believe it until you said it just now. That Mom was going to get better. Something just clicked." His eyes seemed brighter, his smile bigger, and his posture taller.

"I told you I'm always here if you need to talk about *anything*." I winked at him.

"Oh come on, Arianna. Do you always have to make everything about girls?" He shook his head in disappointment.

"How did you know I was going to ask you if you liked anyone?" I gasped.

"The same way you know that I'm not going to wake up for you in the morning," Sam smirked. "It's obvious."

I rolled my eyes and leaned my head against the wall behind me. "You're so immature, Sam."

He pointed to himself and raised his eyebrow in surprise. "You're accusing me of reading your mind and *I'm* the immature one?"

"Well, haven't you heard of twin telepathy?" Of course, all twins knew what the other one was thinking because they were born with a basic instinct to read each other's minds.

"You're right. That's a mature way to look at life." He rolled his eyes and went back to picking at his plate of chicken.

Realizing I had done my job as the nosey twin sister, I got up from the table and walked toward the door. Before leaving I said to Sam in my most serious and calm voice, "Seriously, Sam, if you need to talk about anything I'm always here."

CHAPTER 27

The two weeks after Mom's first treatment went by quickly. Mom was reacting well to the chemotherapy, and despite random nausea attacks and being tired, she seemed pretty much normal.

It was time for her second treatment. After that, all her hair fell out, so she walked around the house with a scarf on her head.

After school, I walked into Mom's room to tell her about my day. To my surprise, she was alone watching TV and reading a book at the same time. "Hi," I said as I sat down on my twisty chair.

She looked up from her book. "Hi."

She looked beautiful. The scarf emphasized her cheekbones—which were extra pointy since she was so skinny—but I could tell something was bothering her. I didn't know if she felt nauseous or if she was just tired, but the look in her eyes made me nervous.

"Is everything okay?" I asked. She looked at me and put her hand to her head. "You can take it off you know. I'm not afraid to see you bald." The truth was, I wasn't afraid to see her bald. How bald could she be?

"Are you sure? It's just that I've been wearing this thing on my head all day and I just . . ." She sighed and looked at me again. The difference between her skinny face and large brown eyes was huge, and I truly felt bad for Mom.

"Mom," I started, "do you want to take it off?"

She looked at me confused as if I was asking her the craziest question in the world. I giggled, which is something I did mostly when I was nervous. I didn't realize asking Mom a simple question would bring out such nerves.

The truth was, I was scared Mom wouldn't take off the wrap because she felt uncomfortable in front of me. The last thing I wanted was for Mom to feel that way in front of her daughter. I guess I was also a little curious as to what Mom looked like bald. But I was sure she was going to look gorgeous, the way she always did.

I motioned to her head as I spoke. "The scarf. Mom, you can take it off . . . I mean, if you want to."

She closed her magazine and leaned back in her chair. "Really?" She placed her hand on the top of the pink and white cloth that covered her mysterious bald head. "Are you sure?"

"What could be so bad under there?" I leaned back in my chair making the springs squeak.

She laughed and took off the scarf placing it on top of the magazine on her lap. Mom rubbed her neck and rested the back of her head on her hands, watching me with a shy smile as I took her in. At first, I flinched. I was not expecting a *real* baldhead. For the record, Mom's head was bald—completely clear of any hair. Her head was small and white. And even though I was always grossed out watching bald men on TV or on the street, I couldn't help but think that Mom looked cute.

"Mom . . . you're cute." I squealed. I ran over to hug her and added, "But you shouldn't show Mollie yet." My sister would not be ready to see Mom's bald head. Once again, I knew something my siblings didn't. This time, it wasn't something scary like cancer. Mom was sharing something with me because she wanted to and I hoped it was because she felt that I was mature enough to handle the truth this time around, not like when she told me about her boo-boo.

"You don't even know how much better I feel. I just felt suffocated underneath all that cloth." Her eyes twinkled and her smile made her skinny face seem fuller. I could tell how relieved she was by the changed look in her eyes.

I laughed, and then she laughed. It was as if being bald had become the funniest thing in the world. Then a thought popped into my head. "Mom, can I ask you a question?" She nodded. "How were you so sure that everything was going to be okay?"

Her mood suddenly shifted, and she looked at me seriously before saying, "I just knew. . . I'm a little embarrassed to say this now . . . I don't know. Maybe I'm just ashamed but—"

"What happened? You can tell me." I made myself comfortable in my chair, ready for a story.

She seemed to think about it. "Remember the weekend before I was diagnosed when I went to Florida with Mimi and Bobby?" All three of them went on a vacation together a few months ago leaving my siblings, Dad, and me all alone for an *entire* weekend. Needless to say, we all felt abandoned.

I nodded.

"Well, I was sitting on the beach one day, and suddenly a thought came into my head. It was like I knew that something bad was going to happen to me. I even told Mimi how I felt. I just can't believe it came true. I can't believe I ever said that.

"I knew when I came home after I was diagnosed, that I was going to have to change. I couldn't keep thinking that bad things were going to happen. So that's how I knew I was going to be okay because I said that everything was going to be okay. I said that I was going to survive. And now, after everything that's happened to me, I'm still here." Mom's face brightened when she smiled. It was like she was realizing the reason why she had cancer in the first place. Was it to realize this? Was it to teach my family we had to be more positive?

"Arianna, did you ever hear the Hebrew word *emunah?*"

"It sounds familiar. What does it mean?" I didn't want to give away the fact that I barely paid attention in Hebrew language class.

"It means faith, sweetie. I know it's cliché, but if you have *emunah*, if you think positively, if you believe that good things will happen. I am starting to believe that they can happen. I call it The Secret."

I twisted my head to face her. I was confused. What was she talking about now? "I completely understood where you were going with this. I just don't get, umm, what's 'The Secret'?"

"Daddy and I call it The Secret. It's our code word for *emunah*. You can use it for anything… parking spots, tests, surgeries, or before chemo. Good things are going to happen, Arianna, we just have to believe that they will," she explained.

"So if I believe that good things will happen then good things will always happen? Then there will be no bad things in the world . . . like, ever?"

"No. Bad things can *always* happen, but maybe if we think good things will happen, we can feel happier and have it easier when we're in a tough situation. Does this make sense?"

"Sort of. I think I get it." But the confused look on my face gave me away.

"Come here." Mom patted the fluffy footstool next to her. I sat there and draped my legs over her. She tickled the bottom of my feet while she spoke. "Tell me about the good things that happened to you today." So I told her about the good things, and she told me about her day.

After that, I started to get The Secret, but I also realized I was probably too young to fully understand Mom's revelation. I wasn't too young, though, to recognize Mom was changing. That meant my family was going to change with her.

Before I left to go to sleep, I rubbed Mom's bald head and kissed it. I reminded her, "Make sure to keep your head clean."

I was extremely happy. I felt so much closer to her than I had in a while. Surgeries and chemo had taken over her life, and I felt I had lost my place. But I felt better because I knew two things: she felt comfortable being around me, and I knew about The Secret.

Before I went to sleep, Sam came into my room. I asked him how he was doing with math, and he said he was doing better, and that he had asked his teacher to give him extra work for extra credit. I told him I had a secret to help him do better on the next test. I made him lean in close before I said, "You should rub Mommy's head."

He crinkled his nose and I knew before he even said anything that the thought of Mom being bald disgusted him. He couldn't even admit that she was sick until recently so I didn't think he would want to see what the chemo was doing to Mom.

"I love her and all, but why would I *ever* do that?"

I smiled. "Didn't you ever hear that rubbing a bald head brings good luck?"

CHAPTER 28

"Mom, can someone drive me to Hailey's house tomorrow afternoon so we can do our project?" I said as I walked into her bedroom before I went to school the next morning.

"Not tomorrow. You know I have my third chemo treatment tomorrow afternoon." She was watching the news, and Dad was getting dressed for work.

"So no one's going to be home for me?" I folded my arms across my chest.

"Bobby will be home when you get home, but she can't leave your brother and sister alone in the house. Can't Hailey come here?"

"Do we have any crayons and markers?" I asked. "I don't think so."

I stormed out of Mom's room. Once again, cancer was taking over my life, and nothing, not even chemotherapy, was able to stop it from spreading. I didn't care about what I had learned from Mom the night before. I didn't care about The Secret.

A half-hour later, I had thought of all the different ways to tell Hailey I couldn't come over tonight. I was petrified to tell her I couldn't go to her house later. But could she really be mad? After all, it was just a project, and she could just bring her supplies over to my house, right?

With my luck, when I walked into the classroom, she came right over to me and squealed the way she always did. "Hey. How's your mom? I'm so excited about tonight. I was thinking of all the different directions we could take this. You know how excited art makes me."

I went straight for it. "Hailey, I don't think I can come over tonight. My mom's getting chemo today, and no one can drive me over." I was organizing my stuff on my desk so I didn't have to look at her face. But when she didn't answer I looked up at her.

"Are you serious? Can't you figure something out?" Her eyes narrowed and I looked for an ounce of sympathy in her eyes. I couldn't find any.

"No. I can't. You know how it's been around my house . . . Crazy." Suddenly, I was angry with her. I had confided in her up until this point and, up until this point, Hailey had been by my side. Now, she suddenly didn't understand.

"I can't deal with this anymore," Hailey said putting her hand on her forehead.

"Deal with what?"

"The fact that you're always sad and moping around because of your mom," Hailey said as she looked at her hands. I stared straight at her, shocked by what she was saying. I wished I were in a dream and when I woke up I'd be alone in my bed instead of standing in front of my best friend who was betraying me. But I wasn't in a dream. Hailey was in front of me and her words were real.

I didn't answer her and for a moment there was silence between us.

But she wasn't finished. "I'm not going to get a bad grade on this project." And my mouth dropped as she said, "Just because *your* mom has cancer."

I looked into her eyes at that moment and they were firm and watching me. Nothing told me that she regretted what she had said and that's what hurt me the most. I needed to get away from her.

"I can't . . ." I couldn't speak. Her words knocked the wind right out of me, and I couldn't breathe. I felt suffocated standing next to her like she was taking all of the oxygen out of the room by making everything—*my* Mom's cancer—all about her. I could not believe she said that to me. I thought she would always be there for me. She told me she understood. She listened to me cry about Mom and her breast cancer, so where did this come from?

"I've got to go," I said to her and left her standing by my desk. I had nothing left to say to Hailey so I went to the bathroom, a place I knew all too well, and started to cry. I missed my entire first class, but I always had a good excuse. My mom had cancer.

I thought very hard about what Hailey said, and I tried to give her the benefit of the doubt. I really did. Maybe she hadn't meant it, or maybe she had a bad morning and got out on the wrong side of the bed. I tried to channel my inner positivity and use The Secret to help make things better but, at first, nothing happened.

Hailey and I ignored each other all day, so it was one of the longest days ever. Our friends must've thought something was up because they went to the back of the classroom during recess to play cards without asking Hailey or me. I guessed they didn't want to get in the middle of whatever was going on or they didn't want our bickering to get in the way of their card game. Either way, I spent most of the day alone and from the looks of it, so did Hailey.

But by the time I got home from school, I wasn't angry with Hailey anymore. To help me get through the day, I'd been trying to think of all the good things Hailey had helped me with instead of focusing on the horrible things she'd said. She had been a great friend, always. Well, except for today. I decided something must've happened that made Hailey feel the way she did and I wasn't going to hold it against her anymore.

Before sitting down at the dinner table, I called Hailey. I checked the clock making sure she'd been dropped off by the bus and she'd be home when I called. I dialed her number and waited for an answer on the other line.

"Hello?" I asked hesitantly. I hoped it wasn't one of Hailey's parents. I hated having the awkward conversation you had with a friend's parent before asking to speak to their kid.

"Ari?" It was Hailey. I sighed in relief.

"Hi."

"Hi."

Silence.

"I'm sorry about today," I started.

"You're sorry? I was horrible to you. I shouldn't have said that. It's just that, um, I guess, um, I don't know. You haven't been yourself lately. I mean you're still so much fun to hang out with, but I never know what kind of mood you're going to be in anymore. Sometimes your sad and don't want to hang out and sometimes you're all in, like when you helped Zoe with Eva."

"I know I've been distracted this year but, I mean, can you blame me?"

"No, and I've tried to be there for you—"

"And you have been. You've been the *best* friend through all of this." I wanted her to know how amazing she had been to me. I hadn't even realized she was becoming upset with me because she always just focused on what I had to say and why I was feeling sad. "You've always listened to me, and I guess I should've realized that it also hasn't been fair to you that I've been so sad all year. And I'm sorry for making everything all about me."

"But I don't want you to think that I didn't want to help you. I guess, I was just getting frustrated and it took over me and made me say those horrible things." She breathed heavily into the receiver and I could sense her frustration shedding.

"You've helped me so much, Hailey. I really couldn't have gone through all of this without you."

Bobby, Sam, and Mollie came into the kitchen and sat down at the table. I had to speed things up if I ever wanted to eat dinner, and I also didn't want them to hear my conversation with Hailey.

"Hailey, thank you for everything."

I heard her smiling into the phone. "I'm sorry, Ari."

There was silence for a minute and I put a finger up to Bobby as if to say, "one minute."

"Can I come over later so we can do our project?" Hailey asked. "If you still want to be my partner."

"Not even the smartest girl in class would be a better partner than you." She giggled into the phone.

"Hey, am I not the smartest girl in class?" I joked.

I could sense Hailey rolling her eyes. "Perfect. I'll go ask my mom when she can drive me and, don't worry, I'll bring the markers."

"Sounds like a plan," I said and thanked her again for understanding before hanging up and joining my family at the kitchen table.

"So you and Hailey are fighting?" Sam asked curiously.

"Dinner's going to be ready in five minutes," Bobby said while tying an apron with a picture of a chef's hat around her waist.

"Thanks," Mollie said.

"Don't start with me, Sam. I had a great day and I don't want you ruining it."

"Well, that's great, Ari," Bobby said from behind the fridge door. "Why don't you tell me about it?"

"I had a great day, too," Mollie piped in.

"Of course you did," I said to her and put a hand on her shoulder. If I had a great day, then she was also going to have one.

Sam banged his head on the table for dramatic effect. "I don't get you guys sometimes."

"Girls," I corrected him and he sighed heavily.

When Bobby finally finished preparing dinner, we all sat together and talked about our day and why it was so great. It was a day I would never forget—it was the first day I channeled The Secret, and I felt *so* good.

CHAPTER 29

The day of my camp appointment was exactly a week after Mom's third chemotherapy treatment. That morning I said, "Mom, I do *not* need a camp appointment this year. They're for four-year-olds who don't know how to match their clothing." I pointed to my outfit to show her how capable I was of dressing myself.

Truthfully, I just didn't think Mom could handle sitting in Denny's, the local clothing store, all day long watching me try on shorts, T-shirts, jeans, sweatpants, pajamas, and anything else I would need for sleepaway camp. It would be a whole day of shopping for everything I needed for camp in *one* day.

I was sure Mom would not enjoy it, especially since she'd be wearing her wig the entire time, and hot flashes and vomit threatened to explode at any moment. And chemo already made Mom tired, so what would shopping do? I didn't want to find out. But Mom insisted this year was just like any other, and we *had* to go to Denny's. She topped it off by saying it would "make her life easier." At that, I stopped fighting and agreed to go. How bad could the day turn out?

After getting dressed, I went into Mom's room to see what wig she decided to wear. Even though she thought they were uncomfortable, I was always amused by the fact she could easily change her hairstyle. She went with the short wig, and she topped it off with her pink barrette. She looked like a little schoolgirl from Paris. I was happy she didn't look as sick as she did sometimes.

"If you don't feel well, we can leave early. Bobby said that she would take me shopping another day," I told her as we walked to the car. Mom made a face. Was I crazy for worrying she wouldn't feel well after receiving three treatments of chemotherapy?

"I'll be fine," she said with confidence and turned the car on. She backed out of the driveway. "Let's just get everything that we need so we can be done, and then I'll just have to focus on Mollie and Sam."

"Yeah right. You're never getting Sam to go to the store." Sam hated shopping. Even when Mom went shopping for him and brought the clothing home for him to try on, he refused. It was like he expected the clothing to magically fit him.

"And I thought my biggest problem was having cancer." Mom laughed to herself as she drove. Even though I felt that it was a little too early for jokes, I laughed along with her, anyway.

After stopping for breakfast, Mom and I eventually pulled up in front of Denny's. We walked inside, and I immediately felt like I was in my element. While I wasn't a *fashionista* or anything, I did love to try on and buy clothing. I had a very difficult time saying no when it came to clothes.

"Hi, my name is Helen." A young sales clerk came over to us and stuck her hand into Mom's face. Then she bent down to say in my face, "And you must be Arianna?"

"You can call me Ari."

"All right, Ari. So we have a lot to do today." She looked around. "Where do you want to start?"

There were a lot of different sections in the store—undergarments, day clothing, night clothing, pajamas, and bathing suits. My head spun just thinking of all the things we needed to buy before camp.

"Let's start with shorts." I pointed to that section of the store. We walked toward it, officially beginning my camp appointment.

Two hours later, Mom and I were running through the store behind Helen, catching all of the clothing she threw at us. She was yelling, "Try this!" and, "Let's grab a smaller size in these!" and, "Aren't these cute?" She clearly wanted me to try on the *entire* store. When she brought us to the dressing room, our pile of clothing was so large it couldn't fit inside. Mom and Helen had to sit outside to watch me try on everything we'd collected.

I was putting on my very own fashion show. I tried on each outfit and modeled it outside the dressing room. Depending on their reaction, I would throw the clothing into a yes, no, or maybe pile.

"Should I be nervous that the 'yes pile' is growing faster than the other piles?" I asked Mom as I strutted down my runway. I kept my eyes focused in front of me the entire time, my arms locked, and my hips swinging. I was channeling my inner model.

When Mom didn't answer I looked at her face for the first time since we began shopping—like really looked at her. I was in shock for a second, and I stumbled on my catwalk.

"Mom, are you feeling all right?" I ran toward her. Her face was so pale, and I saw beads of sweat running down her forehead. It was my fault. Shopping was too much for her, and she wasn't feeling well because of *me*.

She didn't seem as concerned and swatted my hand away. "I'm fine, just tired and hot. Keep going, sweetie." She tried to look happy and excited, but I could see through her act. She wanted to be in bed. I couldn't blame her.

"Maybe we can finish this another day. We have so much to try on, and I should get home," I tried to think of a fast and believable excuse, "to study for a test." Then I looked at Helen. "Would that be okay?"

Helen looked at me with confusion. She probably wasn't used to people leaving in the middle of a camp appointment. Everyone usually wanted to get them over with in one day, since that was kind of the point. She scratched her head and looked around at the mess I had made. Then she started to nod as if convincing herself that she could make this work. "Yes. I'll, um, hold all these items for you for a few more days. Just give me a call when you're ready to continue your appointment." With that, she shook my hand, patted Mom on the back, picked up all of our clothing, and walked away.

"I guess we can go home now," Mom shrugged and walked through the store and out the door. I walked behind her to make sure she didn't fall.

Once outside, Mom gained a little color back on her face. I guess she needed some fresh air. She turned to me and said, "My head was so itchy, Ari. I couldn't sit there anymore."

"I know. It's fine, though. I have a lot to do anyways." We got into the car and before she turned on the engine Mom asked, "Do you mind if I take off my wig?"

"You want to drive bald?" I blinked twice in shock.

Being bald at home was one thing but being out in pure daylight with a bald head wasn't normal. By the look on Mom's face, she was serious. I told her to go for it. I wanted to see the reaction of passing drivers when they saw her driving bald.

"Wait, what test do you have tomorrow?" she asked as she removed her wig and placed it on my lap. I stared at it. She sighed as relief spread across her face. "That feels *so* much better."

"Um, science," I answered nervously. I didn't have a test. I just needed an excuse to get her out of the store.

Mom started driving. "Do you know it yet? If you would have told me you had a test, I wouldn't have let you come today."

BRRIIINNGGGG. Mom pressed the green button on her phone and spoke in her headset. I could always count on the sound of a phone ringing to interrupt me, and I was relieved it happened at that exact moment.

"Hello?" Mom picked up the phone. She laughed and then turned to face me at a red light. "Ari, guess who it is?"

I shrugged.

"It's Mimi. She just passed our car. She called to ask if I'm driving bald."

We burst out laughing.

CHAPTER 30

The night before Mom's last chemo treatment my entire family was sitting in her room talking. Mom was bald. My brother and sister happened to be fine with it. She was sitting on her bed reading a magazine while Mollie and I lay beside her watching TV. Sam and Dad were fighting over a decent show to watch, but they eventually gave up and turned the TV off. They couldn't decide between a comedy and a horror film.

"So after tomorrow, we're done?" Dad asked. He looked at the floor, probably because he didn't know whether mentioning chemo was a good or bad thing.

"Yay!" I leaned in to hug Mom. Then I thought of a brilliant idea and asked, "Wait, what time will you be home?"

"Probably later." She flipped through her magazine.

"Do you think Hailey can come over?" Hailey and I had been waiting for Mom to be out of the house, and I thought I'd found the perfect opportunity.

"Yes. Hailey can *definitely* come over," Sam winked as he walked over to me. I could tell he was trying to annoy me, and it was working.

"Sam, gross, I hate when you talk about my friends like that. They're *my* friends, not yours," I whined.

"Mom, I hate when he does that," I screamed a little too loud in Mom's ear and Mom flinched.

"Ari, calm down." She put on her serious face and rubbed the top of her bald head out of habit. "Yes. Hailey can come over. Now, all of you go to sleep." She was clearly in a bad mood and didn't want to hang out with us anymore. I wondered if she was nervous about tomorrow.

"Mom," Mollie asked. "Are you nervous about tomorrow?" She read my mind.

Mom's face suddenly changed. It went from an I-can't-take-my-kids-anymore type of look to a my-innocent-daughter-needs-me type of look in a matter of seconds. "Why should I be nervous?"

"Isn't it scary?"

"Yes. But I know everything is going to be okay. Right, David?" Dad nodded without looking up from his iPad.

"How do you know?" Mollie said.

"Well, didn't I tell you about The Secret?" Mom's eyes widened when she said those magical words: The Secret. It was like she believed the words saved her.

I took that as my cue to leave. I didn't want to hear Mom explain to my baby sister what it meant to believe that everything was going to be okay when things haven't gone our way. It's not that I cared Mom was telling her about The Secret. I was happy for Mollie to learn what it was, as long as I learned what it was before her. I just knew she would ask a million questions just like any other little kid would. So I walked out of the room and, unfortunately, Sam followed me out.

"Good night, Arianna," Sam called.

I slammed my door shut in response.

When we got home from school the next day, Hailey and I raced up to Mom's room. We ran to one of the closets next to her bed and opened it. When we looked inside, we found exactly what we were hoping to see. All three of her wigs sat peacefully and beautifully on top of the white foam faces. My body buzzed with excitement.

When Mom first bought her wigs, I felt guilty she was wearing fake hair—like she was trying to be someone else. But then Hailey and I wondered what it would be like to try on the wigs and play dress up. We knew we couldn't do that when Mom was around. She'd freak. And she also always wore my favorite one that I'd been dying to try on—the short, Audrey Hepburn-looking one. Today Mom was at chemo, and she always wore a scarf when she went, so this left an open window for Hailey and me to make our dream come true.

I grabbed the short wig off of the foam head and put it on my head. It felt itchy and scratchy against my scalp, and it felt weird wearing something on top of my hair. I looked in the mirror. "Oh my gosh." I couldn't believe my eyes. I was a completely different person. "Hailey, do you see this?" I turned around and looked at Hailey who had put on the long, curly wig and gasped. "You look incredible."

She ran to the mirror and struck a pose. "We should totally get haircuts."

We spent hours ransacking Mom's closets, trying on everything from shoes to dresses to gowns. We created alter egos for ourselves and transformed into *fashionistas* just for the night. But then the phone rang, and my mood shifted. It was Dad updating us about chemo.

"Dad," I said as I picked up the phone. "Everything went okay, right?"

"Yes." He sounded sad. Was he crying? "We're almost there, Ari."

RECOVERY

CHAPTER 31

Mom had started chemotherapy at the beginning of February and finished in the middle of April. After that, we spent Passover in a hotel that was three hours away from our house. It was much different than usual, considering we usually went away to Florida for the holiday, but it was nice being together and not having to worry when the next surgery was or if Mom had to throw up. She was still in recovery, though. I think she always will be.

Mom had to go to the doctor often and had a couple more procedures, but we all knew she was going to be okay. We were so close to the end and my family tried to get things back to normal. That meant we went away for the holidays, had friends sleepover, and threw birthday barbeques.

Mom always loved throwing barbeques, but she did it differently than most people. She always made my dad grill outside but made us eat inside. When we asked her why she always said, "I know that when we go outside to eat, the rain will come out also."

May 19 was my sister's birthday, and Mom didn't want to ruin the traditional birthday barbeques she'd been throwing ever since Mollie turned two. I think Mom felt responsible for causing us to miss out on a lot of birthdays and events while she was sick. And even though she was still recovering and was still bald (though there were tiny black specs on her scalp that meant hair was on its way), she was determined to throw Mollie a birthday party.

We invited my entire family—Mimi and my uncle and their two kids, both sets of grandparents, and all of my cousins. Mollie invited all her friends, and Sam and I were each allowed to invite one of ours. I invited Hailey, of course.

The barbecue was called for the Sunday before Mollie's actual birthday, and when the day finally arrived, Mom's kitchen was in full swing. She was cooking like her old self again.

When it was time to set the table, she asked me to do it. I immediately said yes, happy I didn't have to play with my baby cousins anymore. They were very cute, but they could be annoying. I grabbed plates from the cabinet and walked to the dining room table.

"Where are you going, Ari?" Mom asked looking confused. She was in the middle of frosting a chocolate cake. It looked delicious.

"To set the table? You just asked me to do it."

"Why are you setting it inside?"

I raised my eyebrow out of confusion. "We *always* eat inside."

"Not today. We're celebrating! Set the table outside." She turned all her attention back to her cake.

"But Mom, what if it rains?"

She didn't even look up at me. "It won't."

I didn't fight her. I ran outside to set the table. It had been years since we ate on our porch table.

"Ari, what are you doing?" Dad had taken a break from grilling hot dogs and stared at me.

"Setting the table," I said as if it was the most normal thing in the world. I neatly placed a big fork next to a little fork.

"Why are you setting it outside?" He seemed just as confused as I was a couple of minutes ago.

"Mommy said so," I said it like the reason was obvious.

"Oh." And he started to grill again.

"What?" I looked up from what I was doing. Did he know something I didn't?

He looked at me but didn't say anything. He went back to grilling.

As I placed the cups on the table, I got it. The Secret.

"HAPPY BIRTHDAY TO YOU! HAPPY BIRTHDAY TO YOU!" My entire family stood around the porch watching Mollie gaze at the beautiful *Cinderella* cake before her. There were seven candles on the cake, and she stared with amazement as the fire danced on each one. Everyone was looking at her, watching how she smiled and laughed as everyone sang for her. For the first time in a while, all the attention was on my little sister and only on her. I, on the other hand, stared at the people around me. My family was together, and we were all happy. I honestly never thought that day would come. I thought I would be thinking about cancer for the rest of my life. I thought nothing would ever be okay again. I was wrong.

I watched Mimi, my uncle, and my cousins. They were singing at the top of their lungs and taking pictures that would probably never be developed. I looked at my grandparents. Bobby had tears in her eyes. They'd gone through so much, watching their daughter fight sickness. I looked at Hailey and Sam. I could tell them anything, and they'd always be there.

"HOW OLD ARE YOU NOW? HOW OLD ARE YOU NOW?" we sang.

I looked at Mollie. She had gone through a lot and didn't even completely understand what had happened. I had to ask, "What are you going to wish for?"

She looked at me with her big brown eyes. "I don't know yet. What would you, Ari?"

But there was nothing to wish for. I had everything I needed right in front of me. I looked at my parents, my two favorite people in the world. They'd taught me everything and had been there for me through everything. They loved me and cared for me even when I didn't deserve it and they always will.

Most of all, Mom was amazing. Every morning she woke up and looked at her scars in the mirror. I hoped they didn't remind her of the pain that she went through. I hope they reminded her that she won, that she was one of those survivors now.

I turned to Mollie and said, "Just wish that we're all this happy next year."

Then she blew out the candles.

AUTHOR'S NOTE

Secrets Are No Fun is meant to comfort children who find themselves in a situation others may not understand. When I was dealing with my mother's breast cancer diagnosis, I would have benefited from knowing that others had been through similar experiences.

Many of the characters in this story are fictional, and events and conversations have been compressed and rearranged. My story and emotions described, however, are true accounts of my experience as I remember them. Looking back, I recognize how lucky I was to have a community of family and friends looking out for me during such a difficult time. It truly takes a village to raise a child—and to write a book.

I want to thank my family (my parents, grandparents, aunt, uncle, and cousins… you know who you are) and friends for listening to me talk about writing a book for the last ten years without ever seeing a result. To those of you who painfully read and helped edit my earlier drafts, I extend my deepest gratitude. I love you all very much. To my husband, thank you for pushing me to be brave and publish my story. To my son, one day you'll enjoy books other than *Brown Bear*, and I hope you'll like mine. To my readers, thank you for embracing my story. You are not alone.